FROST TO DUST

THE LAST TRITAN, BOOK II

MYRA DANVERS

FOREWORD

Make sure you sign up for Myra's Newsletter so you never miss sexy NSFW art, free things, exclusive deals, and loads of other cool shit you do not want to miss...

Sign up for Myra's Newsletter today!

myradanvers.com/mailing-list

1
———

A dense fog swirled between my ears. Echoing with a distant call to wake, yet mocking my every effort to obey. In my wrists and throat, a lingering ache gnawing at my sinew. Pressing burning kisses to the hurt.

And through it all, white-hot flames lit the dark. Calling me back.

Demanding my return.

When at last I was able to peel my lids apart, it was to find I was curled around myself on a couch, fully dressed. Clad in a black knee-length wrap. Knotted behind my neck, my back left bare all the way to the top of my bottom. Exposed to the chill of a darkened room.

How I had come to be this way, I could not recall.

Blinking, groggy and disoriented, I brushed at the hair sticking to my sweaty brow.

A flash of gold caught my attention.

Manacles.

On *my* skin.

Horror bled through my veins with the return of memory, and with a cry, I clawed at the warm gold only to recoil in pain.

They were deep. The seam between gold and flesh utterly indiscernible, as if melted into my skin. Buried into the meat in such a way that I knew they might never be removed.

"Nooo," I moaned, voice trembling, gaze transfixed to what I couldn't change. There would be no chafing, no getting snagged on clothing, and no itching beneath the gold.

A smooth, cultured chuckle skated across my nape, making me whirl where I sat, fists raised.

"They're quite permanent," the captain said, dark eyes two gleaming pricks of light that watched from across a darkened room. Cruel amusement etched into every line of his face.

I gasped.

Naked from the waist up, hair still damp from the bathhouse—tousled and unruly—his lower half was encased in dark slacks. Muscle rippled as he fidgeted with a length of fabric, watching me without so much as a blink.

"Where am I?" I asked through dry lips.

"We are in the master bedroom of the house I occupy, in what used to be Elora," he replied, closing the distance between us with a slow, relentless roll of his hips.

Heat flared across my cheeks. "Don't touch me," I hissed, and pressed my back to the couch.

He hummed through a smirk. "Ah, but I own you, Mila. It is my right to do whatever I damn well please with my property."

"You don't own me," I snapped, baring teeth. Braced for the invasion of my personal space. Straining *not* to see the shape of long fingers, to remember the press and slide—

"Mmm," he purred, stepping too close. Enough that his heat touched my collarbones. "And *that* sounds like a challenge."

"It shouldn't," I hissed, and hopped onto the back of the couch. Crouched at eye level, knuckles white— until he straightened, towering above me.

"Such a saucy mouth," he crooned, grinning now. "I can think of plenty of things to keep those pretty lips of yours busy."

In response, I merely showed him my teeth. A silent dare for him to put something delicate in my mouth.

He lunged for my arm with a bark of cold laughter, but I was ready.

Throwing my weight in the opposite direction, I made a beeline for the door.

"Oh, Mila?" he sang, and in an instant, my every muscle seized stiff and solid against my will.

A fine tremor rippled through my body, but no matter how hard I tried to struggle—to fight or flee—I was frozen.

In my wrists and throat, a burning tingle that tasted of dark flames. Ravenous, burning frost that buried pointed teeth deep into my marrow and supped on my life force. Gulped down great, heaving swallows of my energy before I had a chance to do more than sense it going to support another.

Stolen.

Warm fingers skated down the length of my exposed spine. Bumping over the ridges—a shiver the only movement I was allowed.

His voice was a soft, cultured hum of debauchery and threat when he asked, "Would you like to learn why your cuffs are called '*Tritan chains*' when there are no chains in sight?"

With my back to the captain, I hadn't a choice but to stand utterly still. Held perfectly immobile, he left me trembling in the center of his bedroom, my body no longer mine to control. Jaw locked tight, for his question was rhetorical.

"Look at your wrists for me, darling."

My head bowed and my gaze dropped, and though I tried with all my might to deny the command, I couldn't help but look.

Glowing.

Bright light burning without heat, the cuffs encircling my wrist were blazing with a brilliance that made my eyes water. But it wasn't the complete inability to move, nor the threat of what the captain might do with this absolute control.

It was my skin.

Standing rigid beneath the surface, tracing a handspan away from the manacles, my veins were illuminated with the pulse of molten gold.

Asher, infecting my very blood with his tainted, Caledonian influence.

He stepped around me, strolling into my line of vision. "Beautiful, isn't it?" he asked, and dragged the back of his knuckles down my cheek. And then, with a ravenous smirk, he lifted his wrist to show off the matching cuff fused to his skin. A golden circlet glowing with *my* energy. "They allow me to control you," he murmured. "I can stop you from running with nothing more than a thought." One finger on my chest, he pushed me back. "I can have you drop to your knees and worship my cock like a seasoned whore," he continued, herding me toward the couch against my will. "And I can make you like it, though"—he smirked—"that comes from experience, not the chains."

Panic bubbled up between my ribs, and as if he wanted to hear the desperation in my voice, he released my jaw enough to allow me to say, "Please don't," in scarcely more than a whisper. Shamed into begging.

Into being *allowed* to beg.

A laugh bubbled up from deep inside his chest, and he said, "Sit," through that vile smirk that only widened when I obeyed without a moment's hesitation. "Believe me, pet," he drawled, and slid one hand up, around the curve of my hip and beneath the cushion—under the scraps of black silk—to cup the sensitive meat of my bottom. "You'll beg. And it will be beautiful."

Head falling back, I spat, "I won't beg to be raped," through pointed teeth. Letting him feel every bit of my hatred. My helpless wrath.

He watched as my thighs fell apart at the slightest, coaxing touch, then settled between them. One knee pressing against my core, he stooped. Pressed his lips to my neck, teeth rasping over throbbing, delicate flesh. "Do you think the pleasure slaves throw themselves at my feet because I abuse them?" he whispered against my ear, and sent ice shivering through my blood. "Because I force them?"

But in spite of myself, I sneered. Goaded into bickering, despite the way my heart hammered behind my ribs. "You're right. A good whipping really is the best way to a woman's heart."

A wicked grin flicked against the corner of my jaw. "Your heart holds no interest to me, slave," he murmured, and set his knee to rock against the place where I ached. "And I already have what I *need* from you."

"I'll die before I service you or your men," I

snarled, trapped beneath him. Unable to so much as lift a finger against his influence. Helpless to the whims of cruelty or mercy. Tormented by the wicked lust flickering in those inky, Caledonian eyes.

Amusement lapped at my senses. Foreign and dark and obliterating my indignant fury, he possessed me. Completely. Filled me with elite energy and left me gasping and disoriented. "You belong to me now, Mila. And I don't share."

Tears flooded my lash line, but I clung to the only thing I had left. Snark. "Says the man with a harem of public sex slaves."

"Purchased for the men I command."

"That's the very definition of sharing!"

He laughed before pressing his lips to mine. Stealing my breath, my voice. Every last drop of my sense.

"What I mean to say is that I shall not be sharing *you*." His influence faded away before I could muster a response, leaving me free to squirm. To fight with more than words and wit. "Come," he said, and pushed off the couch, retreating into an ensuite bathroom without a backward glance. "We'll be late for supper."

I scrubbed at my arms, my throat and wrists, trying to shake the feeling of Captain Asher Rawlings crawling through my blood and sinew. Learning everything that I was from the inside out. And, voice shaking, I said, "I'm not hungry," through a curled lip.

"And I wasn't asking."

He reappeared, wearing a black suit that hugged his muscular frame. Glittering with the stars and pins that denoted his rank within the Caledonian army. For a moment, he simply took me in. Dark eyes narrowed, flicking over my clenched fists, my spread, braced feet. And then, "Don't spoil my good mood with a fight you can't win, Mila. I can promise you won't like the consequences."

I laughed, despite the tears fogging my vision. "What more can you do to me? You can't kill me—I'm the source of your newfound power. Probably the very last free priestess, which means you'll *never* have another chance like this," I said, gaining confidence with every spoken word. Enough that I dared stalk toward him in my temper. "I can heal any damage you do to my body because I no longer have anything to hide. So go ahead. You can't hurt me, *elite*."

For the space of several breaths, there was nothing. Only the quiet sounds of a one-sided power struggle.

And then, "That you think so is oddly... refreshing. The opinion of a sheltered, naive little girl, of course, but refreshing nevertheless. And tempting as it might be to teach you the errors in your thinking, I'm due at General Tilcot's manse at the top of the hour." He paused then, fidgeting with a golden button at his wrist, shaking his head as if amused by my passion. "Let me offer you some advice, given that

I'm in something of a celebratory mood. Go out of your way to behave yourself in the company of these men. Under no circumstances are you to draw attention to yourself, do you understand me?"

I laughed, sneering. "Will my bad behavior reflect poorly on you?" I cooed, lightheaded with the rush of being near such a villain. The deadly push and pull I wasn't sure I'd survive. Wasn't sure I could muster the effort to care, given all I'd lost.

One large, rough hand settled on the back of my neck, and I was made to still as he caught my gaze in the bottomless, inky swirl of dark eyes. He said, "Yes," in such a way that saw my snide retort whither on my tongue. Held rapt and attentive. "Owning a priestess is a privilege. One that can be taken away without impacting my status as an asset to the empire."

It was my turn to grin, and I let him see the savage point of my teeth. "So I *can* be rid of you, then? I can break this infernal bond and—"

"You mistake me," he said, and closed what little distance there was between us. Chest to chest, looming above me in a way that made me feel tiny. Fragile and insignificant. "I don't need to be *in possession* of my priestess to be an asset to the empire. That is, to use your power to kill rebel scum." He cupped the back of my neck and let a rough thumb skate over my cheek, beneath my eye before his fingers tangled in the fine hairs at my nape. "They can hide any embarrassing assets away in the capital. Locked away in a cell, where no one will ever think to wonder after your health. Where it doesn't matter that you're bound to me, or that I have no intention of sharing that sweet little pussy with a garrison of my men." His fingers grew tight with warning. "There are things you've never thought to be terrified of, Mila. Horrible things that would see you begging to take my cock. To please me in any way your pretty little head can dream up, for nothing at all, except the promise that you'll remain in *my* care. So *yes*, Mila. Your bad behavior will reflect poorly on me, but *you* will pay the higher price." He released me, then. Took a quick breath and stepped back, raking one hand through thick, dark hair. "But there's only one way to break this bond."

"A-and what's"—I cleared my throat—"What's that?"

He shrugged, dark eyes glittering and heavy with warning. "You'll have to die."

2

———

A hard lump of bile rose to the back of my throat as the reality of his words sank in.

Knowing just what he'd stolen from me with three bands of gold.

My life. My power. *Everything* that I was...

... all tied to Captain Asher Rawlings.

Forever.

A fragile whisper spilled over my lips. Helpless denial of a thing I *knew* to be true. "You're lying."

Some complicated emotion flicked across his brow, but he shrugged. Held himself in tight control before I could make sense of it. "Perhaps. But are you so willing to take the risk?"

Incredulous, I swallowed around the lump strangling my voice, and said, "You expect blind trust?"

He smirked, closing the distance between us once more. Flexing his influence to force me still, just because he could, the captain adjusted the vulgar scraps of black silk hanging from my shoulders. Knuckles *almost* brushing my nipples when he said simply, "I expect obedience from my pet, and know just how to extract it, don't I?"

My cheeks grew warm at little more than the reminder of what he'd done to me. What he'd made me do, bent over his desk.

Naked.

Spread—a feast to his depraved whims.

Nothing between us but rough fingers and whispered promises of things I couldn't even begin to imagine until he was forcing me to learn.

To feel and obey.

Tormented by the heart-rending pain of the most intimate of betrayals—that of my own body dancing to the commands of another.

A predator who craved a feast of my fear and anguish.

Disgust made me bold when I might have been bashful, and though my voice trembled, I said, "You're a monster."

He made no effort to deny it. Merely sent his fingers to tangle in my hair, pulling me close before he pressed his lips to my scalp. Inhaling, he took a breath that whispered against my skin.

Possessive. Taking far, *far* too many liberties for his intent to be mistaken for anything but the ravenous, greedy thing it was.

And then I felt it.

The kiss of dark flames, his elite energy came alive in a rush. Licking at the edge of my senses. Tasting what no other might see, he groaned. Pressed deeper and drank me in, his fingers biting where they clenched too hard, he filled me with the reminder of what was now *his* to wield.

My power.

And then, "Well isn't that something," he murmured. Stepping back, he pushed a tangle of fine hairs back from my forehead. Standing too close, he laughed. "It's not often that I find myself mistaken, let alone flat out *wrong*."

Confused, I frowned. "Wh-what—"

A cruel smirk spread over straight, white teeth, and he released me from his influence. Gave me the power to fight when he tipped my chin back. Fingers growing tight where they were tangled at my nape. "You're... tempted."

A hard lump flapped behind my ribs. Confusion an impenetrable fog that coated my tongue.

"No, it's okay. You don't need to say anything, pet." Rough hands framed my face, and he pressed close enough that his lips grazed mine. Not quite tender, it was a threat. "I can sense it," he said. "What you need but can't admit. Not yet."

Heart beating in my throat, I shook my head. "I don't—"

"But we don't have time to indulge just now," he

drawled, thumbs dropping to trace the edge of my collar. Cupping both sides of my throat. "Appointments to keep." He stepped back, and with a click of his fingers that shroud of alien energy fell upon me once more. "Come along."

Teeth bared in helpless fury, I was made to follow when he turned. His influence a tight band that forced me to walk through the halls of his temporary, stolen home. A leash with no slack, keeping me half a pace behind him—where a proper slave might stand in wait.

He left me no option but to look where I could, seething. To breathe and obey, despite the way I lusted after the broad, exposed back displayed before me. Wishing for a lapse in judgement, where I might snatch up something heavy—a weapon, *anything* that could leave a dent in the back of that arrogant skull.

But his control didn't waver.

Not for an instant.

Instead, he took me down a narrow set of stairs, guided me around a corner and passed an intimate, sparse kitchen. I blinked, watching from deep inside his shadow as he threw open the front door and filled my lungs with a gust of refreshing evening air. A soothing breeze that couldn't ease the horror of my feet carrying me into the street at another's command.

Yet despite everything, I was happy to be outdoors again, where the cool evening air washed away the stink of anxiety. The stress of being enthralled to an elite. Of being powerless in a game with rules I had not yet learned.

Pavement cold on my bare feet, I allowed myself a moment to pine for my durable tree bark boots. To wish for the luxury of choice, wondering if I'd ever make another for myself again.

Teeth grinding, I cleared my throat, and through a mask of false bravery asked, "Where are we going?"

He didn't turn. Didn't so much as bother to waste a glance in my direction. "Have I left you with the impression that there will be open discourse between us?"

"No, but I—"

"Then this is the perfect time for another lesson vital to your continued survival here. In the company of their betters, slaves will be seen, not heard."

An incredulous bark of laughter burst from my lips. "Oh, my deepest, most sincere apologies!" I cried, tone rich with reckless, mock outrage—the only rebellion I could manage in my state of forced restraint. "I had no idea us lowly slaves aren't meant to voice our opinions!"

"Keep it up, Mila," he purred, lips crinkled at the edge. Promising all sorts of wickedness I had no way to defend against. No way to brace or prepare.

But for a moment, as I matched his challenge with a glare of my own, I wasn't sure if I cared. Let him show me who he was. Let him feed the hatred that burned, starving for an outlet.

My stomach growled, the distant memory of stale bread echoing with a plea for temperance. To recover my strength if only so I might fight all the harder.

With a hitching breath, I lowered my head. Gaze catching on the uneven cobbles beneath my bare feet.

With a nod, the captain's hand found purchase on my lower back. Calloused palm catching delicate silk, making it pull in such a way that drew sharp awareness to the spots where it grew tight and binding. Hips, ribs... my breasts.

"A slave should be seen, not heard, and speak only when spoken to," he continued, voice a light, taunting rasp. "Understood?"

Teeth clenched, I grimaced at the dark and spat out a bitter, "Yes," through the points of my modified canines—and felt the blunt scrape of his nails where they dragged across my skin. A warning that drew my gaze to his in a snap, where I found his attention already fixed to my face. One brow raised in wait. So, with a sneer, I tacked on a surly, "*Sir*," that held no trace of the respect the designation might otherwise warrant.

It was enough.

"Your arrival here has caused quite a stir," the captain murmured as we drew near a sprawling manse. Sweeping white stone and manicured gardens lined both sides of a grand entrance, the Eloran architecture nothing but an aching whisper of the people who had once lived in this fallen city. "General Tilcot has decided to throw a feast in my honor, but make no mistake. This is nothing more than a pretty trap, just waiting to snap shut."

Before I could ask what he meant, a heavily pregnant, statuesque woman emerged from the front doors in a swirl of silk and gold. "Asher!" she cried, and kissed the captain's cheeks. One after the other, a swirl of midnight locks spilling down her back. "So good to see you darling. And with such a rare creature in tow!"

A heavy shadow emerged over her shoulder.

General Tilcot.

The naked elite who'd stayed to watch me in the baths. Whose eyes had seen everything beneath these flimsy scraps pretending to be clothing.

"Let the poor man get a foot in the door before you throw yourself at him, Tyra," the general said. And then, daring to reach out with a curled knuckle, he caught me under the chin and tipped my head into the light. "My God. Asher, tell me this isn't our filthy little wildcat?"

"*My* filthy wildcat, sir," the captain returned with an easy smile and a possessive hand on my shoulder. His finger twisting in the hair at my nape, he pulled me back a few inches. Enough that I stumbled into his chest. "This is Mila, my Tritan priestess. Say hello, pet," he said, and squeezed the meat above my clavicle.

Instead of obeying, I let my head drop, offering only a tiny, stiff bend at the knee. Avoiding eye contact and affecting an air of subservience in one, defiant action.

"Mila," the general hummed, taking liberties with my silks. Adjusting what did not need fixing, his fingers left a trail of sticky cold disgust in the wake of his touch. "Well, I must say, you look lovely in Caledonian colors, girl. A true prize claimed in the name of the empire." He stooped, leaning in close enough that his breath warmed my cheeks, though his gaze remained fixed over my shoulder. On the captain, a dangerous glint sparkling in those murky depths, his eyes laced with more brown than what was present in the captain's ebon glare. "A prize I'm not sure the young master Rawlings can possibly keep... given all the challenges sure to come his way now that you're bound. And without permission, I might add."

I swallowed, *hard*. Sweat blooming on my brow, the back of my neck—where the captain's touch had grown tight with a nip of biting pain.

But he laughed and said, "I'm sure I'll find a way to manage, sir."

Without another word, the general hummed, slipped his hand around Tyra's waist, and turned to escort us down a long, richly appointed hallway.

Under my breath, I tipped my head in the

captain's direction, and asked, "How was that, Asher? Have you any performance notes?"

At the sound of his name on my lips, he went stiff. Skewering me with a glare that promised retribution, he pressed his lips to my ear. "I wonder if you'll enjoy these little rebellions half as much as I'm going to enjoy breaking you of the habit? Do let me know, won't you?" he cooed, then sent me stumbling down the hall. A mess of fear and fury tangled behind my ribs, veins thick with the urge to sink my teeth into the back of Captain Asher Rawlings' thick neck.

The general guided us down a long hall that opened into a massive dining room. In the center, a heavily laden table dressed in black and gold drapery stretched the length of the room.

One step inside, and I faltered. Shocked still by the sudden onslaught radiating off the forty or so people already seated.

Power.

It struck me with the force of a falling tree. Buried me beneath an avalanche of wet spring snow, trapping me where the air was frozen solid. Where panicked flight was the only reasonable response to such a confrontation.

The Caledonian elites. Gathered together, sipping from crystal goblets, chatting and laughing amongst themselves.

A virtual army of unstoppable killers at rest.

Propelling me forward, a familiar, hated hand

settled on the naked skin of my lower back. "Where's your bravado now?" the captain whispered, and sent a shiver racing through my blood as his lips rasped against my ear. The heat of his chest cloaking the naked skin of my back.

I took another step—and found horror waiting around a towering pillar of white stone.

Bound and gagged, there was a woman spread over a cross. Her limbs a lewd *X* that left her exposed to a sea of powerful men who thought nothing of such a heinous display. Men who sipped wine and nibbled cheese, sending only the occasional appreciative glance toward an expanse of pale flesh laced with angry red stripes.

As if drawn to my presence, she turned her head and my heart leapt into the back of my throat.

The Head Priestess.

Brought low and strung up.

Appearing at my side, the general chuckled. "You've a fine eye for tonight's entertainment, I see. My Sasha is being punished for withholding your identity," the general explained, stepping forward to stroke one long finger down Sasha's back. Tracing the marks, he grinned when she whimpered and squirmed. "You lied to me, Sasha," he murmured. "A few more lashes should cure you of that nasty habit, I think."

She turned liquid blue eyes back, begging for mercy from a man who'd never give it.

I could feel it. The distant echo of fear pouring off her in suffocating waves. The hopeless, desperate plea for help that might never come.

And before a single rational thought could flick through my head, I staggered forward, and cried, "I'll take her punishment!"

Silence fell over the elites, and as one, they turned dark eyes upon me.

"Please," I whispered in a tone meant for the general, but my voice traveled around the room nevertheless. "I-I don't mean to be rude—"

"And yet, here we are," the captain drawled, placing his hand on my arm without exerting his influence.

At his droll comment, the tense spell shattered and the gathered elites laughed. Indulgent smiles gracing several faces, they went back to their chatter. Their sipping and nibbling.

"You've got a long way to go in the training of this one, don't you, Rawlings?" the general purred, though his face held none of the amusement present in his voice. And then to me, "Sasha knows the rules, girl. If she'd been forthcoming, you would be mine now. She cost me the opportunity to be the first elite bound to *two* priestesses, and for that, she will be severely punished."

"But it's not her fault!" I cried, and the captain's fingers grew tight, unyielding.

I slapped his hand away.

"Ah, and there's our wildcat." The general grinned, a hungry gleam entering his gaze as he took me in. Eyes dropping to my chest, before drifting lower. Doing a leisurely sweep of exposed skin no longer stained by walnuts.

Without missing a beat, the captain said, "I find her temperament rather fitting for a man of ambition."

The gathered elites laughed, a polite smattering of applause echoing over the din of chatter. And with that, they descended. Congratulating the captain, inspecting his newest acquisition with greedy touch.

Me.

"You lucky son of a bitch!" one man said, and punched the captain's shoulder. "My priestess cost me almost half a million. How much did you pay, Rawlings? I've heard the rumors, but I don't want to believe them."

A slick grin spread across the captain's lips. "The opening bid was a hundred."

"You paid a *hundred* dollars for a Tritan priestess?"

"No." And the captain's teeth gleamed strong and white, when he added, "I paid fifty."

Cries of shock met his claim, and clutching at his throat, the jealous elite slung his free arm across the captain's shoulders. "I feel sick," he said, leaning heavily on the captain as we were escorted to the large table.

The captain pulled his chair back, an air of smug accomplishment positively oozing from his skin.

But there was no seat for me.

I blinked, shocked. Uncomfortable to be left standing while everyone else had already taken a seat.

And it was at that moment, fidgeting in an ocean of powerful men, utterly out of place, that I noticed the dozens of Tritan women already kneeling at the feet of their captors. Half-hidden beneath the table, eyes downcast, their hands folded in their laps. Knees braced on thin, silky pillows.

But through the reek of the elite, I could feel their fear. Even through the blinding fog that was Captain Asher Rawlings, it permeated the room, making my heart beat faster in horrified empathy.

Tritan's priestesses.

I'd found them.

"Kneel," the captain drawled, but it was laced with something vicious. A dare for me to continue defying him despite his warnings for me to obey.

"Like a dog?" I hissed, outraged.

"No, Mila," he said, and used his influence to force me down. "Like a slave."

3
———

Dinner started with drinks. The elites spoke of the war as if they didn't have the people of a conquered nation at their feet, as if Eloran slaves weren't flitting about, clearing plates and refreshing drinks.

As if a former Head Priestess of the Tritan faith wasn't strapped to a cross, whipped, gagged, and humiliated.

And yet, there I knelt, shaking with so much impotent fury, without even the luxury of the captain's influence to force me still.

He'd released me. Left me kneeling there, smothered in a cloud of arrogant, elite oppression. Knowing I hadn't the courage to defy him in company such as this.

Above me, General Tilcot tossed the remnants of

his glass back, swallowing with a hum. "What happened to your unit, Rawlings? I heard you lost ground."

An indulgent sigh spilled from the captain's lips. "We did," he admitted. "The rebels managed to hit us with a few explosive charges at shift change." He shrugged, though his eyes went flat and hard. Wary, I assumed, of a trap with gilded jaws. "Nothing but a few injured men, though..." Pausing long enough to sip at a tumbler of amber liquid, he added, "It could have been much worse, of course." Absently, he stroked my hair. Gentle, despite the snag of callouses catching at my roots. Making my scalp dance. "Incidentally, that's why I was looking for a new girl in the first place." A sinister chuckle skated along my nape, igniting my temper. "Nothing inspires a soldier to work harder than access to high-quality pussy, which is something my men seem to have forgotten."

"I heard she was a dreadful sight when you got her," said an elegant woman seated across the table. Most of her face left hidden from my vantage point on the floor, until she shifted forward. Inspecting me down the length of a narrow, aristocratic nose. A perfect coil of gleaming, ebon thick hair positioned to cover her right breast. "Was she to be a punishment for your men? Or are the common folk really so desperate that they'll stoop as low as... *that.*"

At this, the captain smirked and turned his attention down. To me. Swirling the amber liquid in his glass, he watched me from eyes gone dark as pitch, and said, "Mila, how long did you live in the forest?"

Insulted, feelings hurt, I let my glare fall to the cushion beneath my knees and mumbled, "I don't know."

The elegant woman sneered. "Honestly, Asher. I don't understand your tolerance for such blatant disrespect. A man of your up-and-coming station deserves much better," she purred, making it impossible for anyone to mistake her intentions toward Captain Asher Rawlings.

"Nonsense, Carina," he returned with a smile, all the while those fingers remained tangled in my hair. Petting... stroking with an absent-minded compulsion. "Mila's testing her limits, that's all. All new slaves need to figure out what they can and can't get away with," he said and refreshed her glass. "Now, Mila, I'll ask again. How old were you when you fled the Empire?"

I shook off his touch with a jerk of my shoulders. "Eighteen."

"And how old are you now?" he purred, and merely continued to stroke through the silky, well-groomed locks he couldn't seem to get enough of.

A sneer curled at the edge of my lips. *"I don't know,"* I said, enunciating every word.

Carina scoffed, but with a patronizing smirk the

captain pressed on. "Let's try something different, hmm? When did you flee Elora?"

Confusion bunched between my brows. "I didn't," I replied. "I'm Tritan"—I seized a handful of that hated, silver-blonde hair, shaking it with a flick of my wrist that glittered with the stamp of gold, the mark of a bound priestess—"remember?"

It was his turn to frown, and he lurched forward to cup my chin in strong fingers. To make me look, when he said, "You left *Tritan*?" with genuine surprise etched across his face. "Mila..." He shook his head. "We conquered Tritan *five years ago*. Have you been in the forest all that time?"

I blinked at the news, but that was all. Concealing my shock behind lax facial muscles and a wall of simmering spite.

The general laughed, boisterous and loud. "Five years of filth would *indeed* be adequate motivation to get results out of the rabble!"

And as if given permission, the rest of the diners followed suit. Elite laughter echoing all around me. Sending heat to flood my cheeks, filling my chest with mortified shame.

"Ah," the general sighed, and sat back. Hands clasped in his lap as a wall of Eloran slaves emerged from the kitchens, laden with trays of steaming food. "Dinner is served."

Stomach rumbling, I couldn't help the way my

mouth watered. The tilt of my head as I tried to catch the scent of Eloran cooking—a beloved staple of my upbringing, and one I was suddenly aching to try again.

But the instant the first silver lid was lifted, my heart plummeted.

"I haven't had a good steak in months," the captain said, grinning at a plate swimming in blood, butter, and garlic.

Dejected, I sank back into my cushion.

"I was getting rather tired of rations myself," another replied. The jealous man, who'd paid half a million for the honor of putting a Tritan priestess on her knees.

"Don't fast on my account!" the general said, flicking his utensils at the elites before cutting into his steak with a flourish. "Dig in."

Resigned to yet another hungry, sleepless night, I scowled at my chains. Digging a fingernail at the seam of gold and flesh, just to feel the nip of pain. To wallow when I was unable to act.

Fingers cascaded through my hair. "I really shouldn't be rewarding your behavior with steak," the captain said, "but you'll need the energy. Eat."

Startled, I glanced up to find the captain's free hand outstretched. Between his fingers, a slab of lightly charred flesh, dripping in grease.

Mouth flooding with sour spittle, I cringed back

and said, "No, thank you, sir," with all the learned courtesy of a high-born, Tritan lady.

The captain sighed, one brow cocked as he pinned me with a dark glare. "Must you fight me at every turn?" He pushed the strip of steak closer to my lips. Insistent. "Eat."

"Sir, I'd really rather not," I whispered, trying to convey my disgust. To beg him for mercy in this, if nothing else.

"And as I've already made clear, I don't care what you'd *rather* do, Mila. Eat, or I'll strap you up on the cross beside Sasha."

I lurched back, scrambling to a ready crouch, and hissed, "Then I'll take the whipping!"

For a moment, the captain was silent as I scowled at the offensive offering. Sweat beading across my brow as our whispered argument began to draw unwelcome attention.

And then, "What issue could you possibly have with steak?" the captain asked, baffled enough that his glare grew soft and hazy with confusion.

I swallowed, cheeks heating as I tried to hold his gaze. "I don't eat meat."

A cold bark of laughter burst from his lips. "You mean to tell me you're a vegetarian with teeth like *that*?"

"Please..." Creeping forward, I dared to touch his ankle. Content with playing the submissive if it meant I might win this one small battle. "*Please...*

don't make me eat it," I whispered, staring at him with what might pass for reverence. Artful tears pooled along my lash line, threatening to spill down my cheeks. The very picture of fragile femininity.

Something wicked gleamed at the back of his eyes, and he stroked the side of my face with calloused fingers. "Mmm. It's not quite the begging I had in mind, but beautiful nevertheless. Unfortunately," he said, "what you eat is no longer your concern. We can talk about your dietary privileges when you learn to behave."

A sneer shattered my dainty mask, and without bothering to hide my disdain, I said, "Over my stinking, bloated corpse."

"It seems," the general hummed, watching me down the length of his nose, "our wildcat needs a touch more than idle threats to garner true obedience."

The captain went stiff, his touch growing tight and hot where it sank into the meat of my shoulder.

"But what to do," the general mused, setting his utensils aside, "for the slave who doesn't fear physical repercussions, hmm?" He laced his fingers together and hid a smirk behind steepled fingers. "A slave so willing to throw herself in harm's way can't be controlled with mere threats of violence. Oh, no. She needs a stronger hand. Something precious to lose, for the little martyr who'd sacrifice herself to spare another." He clapped those large hands, and drew the attention of every last man and slave present in the dining hall. "Ah, of course"—he cast about, scanning the room as if lost in thought—"Captain Rawlings, every moment of further disobedience from our girl earns... *Sasha* ten lashes. I feel that's fitting, no?"

"N-no!" I cried, aghast. Horrified and cold, right down to the middle.

"No?" The general smirked, and it was a predatory thing that made the hair at my nape bristle. "Twenty, then. Unless you'd prefer thirty? Though"—dark brows climbed toward the general's hairline—"I'll admit, I'm growing leery of your thirst for seeing my Sasha marked! Quite the vicious little thing we've got, Asher my boy!"

Nausea swirled in my gut, burning the back of my tongue. And for a moment, I could do little else but sit and stare. Unblinking. Unable to breathe under the weight of such cruelty.

Utterly without options.

Swallowing a sob, I snatched the soggy bit of meat from the captain's fingers and popped it into my mouth without giving myself a moment to really think.

Warm.

Juicy.

A chunk of fatty grizzle crunched between my molars.

I gagged, eyes squeezed shut. Stomach heaving at the sensation of bloody, half-cooked flesh sliding down the back of my throat. Of sinew caught between my teeth. The rich scent that invaded my sinuses and left a film of grease thick and tacky on my lips.

"Oh, come on, Mila!" the captain said, his laugh a deep rumble of pure amusement, echoed by the rest of the elites and their women. "It's not half as bad as all that!"

I swallowed.

Heaved.

Swallowed again, and pulled a breath through gaping jaws. "I hate you," I whispered, low enough that no one but *he* heard above the ringing laughter.

But he merely smirked, placing another slice of steak on his tongue, eyes closing on a groan of pleasure. Mocking me.

I gagged again, panting, the taste still lingering on my pallet. And, violated in a way I had never thought possible, angry tears threatened to spill over my lashes.

But I'd done it. Without complaint.

Sasha wouldn't be torn up by an elite with a whip, cursing my name through tears and a gag.

"Mila, darling." He said it in a song. The captain cooing in the tone of one already drunk on victory. Gloating.

Breath catching, I turned watery eyes up to find his fingers already laden with another strip of steak.

One rarer than what had come before. Thicker with glossy ribs of muscle severed with a serrated blade.

With trembling fingers, I reached for the next bite.

"Ah," he breathed, and pulled it back. "No, pet. Slaves take nourishment from their master's hand."

Incredulous, I met his eye—and shivered at what I saw there.

The hunger.

A thing I recognized from that night in his office. Something I'd felt in the slick glide of work-hard fingers, in the ragged breath on my nape as he—

Unable to break from the look in those inky black depths, I leaned forward. Plucking the steak from his fingers with the edge of pointed teeth. Careful not to touch his skin. Not to encourage the flare of elite flames looking for fuel.

Chewing as fast as I could manage, I swallowed it nearly whole and choked when it stuck in my throat.

But the captain would not be deterred. "Lick," he purred when my tongue lolled out in distress.

I shook my head, staring at the bend in my knees. At the dark silk of the pillow placed there just for me. In anticipation of my surrender.

His touch landed on my lips, leaving the choice to me.

Obey, and swallow the taste of my unsalvageable dignity as it was left in pitiful tatters, or bear the weight of Sasha's whipping—and be forced to eat the meat anyway.

Smothering a sob, I took his fingers into my mouth and sucked until they were clean. Until all I could taste was salt and man. Straining not to think of where those fingers had been, what they'd done...

What they'd made me do.

"Good girl," the captain rumbled, tilting my chin back so I might see the need smoldering in his eyes and know he was remembering too.

Planning.

He continued to feed me as the evening progressed, taking care to pass me dainty, bite-sized strips. Insisting I lick his fingers clean between morsels, while I tried *not* to make a meal of his flesh and bone. To think only of Sasha and the leverage the general wielded with such careless ease.

It wasn't long before the dull thrum of conversation faded into the background. Before something deep inside me began to revolt against the surge of fatty protein churning in my gut. My ears were ringing, my cheeks flushed and hot, and when a fist of pain blossomed in my stomach, it was with a profound knowledge that all hope for salvaging what remained of my dignity had run dry.

"Drink," the captain said with a frown. Mild concern etched across that dark brow.

With trembling fingers, I accepted the glass, draining it in one long pull.

Carina rolled her eyes, ankles crossing beneath the table. The flash of red heeled shoes sparkled beneath the table. "Are all your slaves this much work?"

"No," he replied with a laugh. "It seems Mila will require a significant amount of attention, but then, she isn't one of my regular slaves, is she?"

A cold sweat broke out on my brow, signaling imminent disaster. And with trembling fingers, I tapped the captain's thigh once more.

He brushed my hand away.

"You know," Carina said, licking the full bow of her lower lip. One of those red heels darting between his ankles, only to slide up. A slow caress that glided from the captain's ankle to his knee. Inching closer to his inseam. "I've never understood the appeal of owning a pleasure slave."

"No?" he answered, offering a bland smile.

Shaking her head, Carina sipped at her drink. "A man of a conquered nation couldn't possibly compare to a full-blooded Caledonian, much less an *elite*," she purred. And then, as Eloran slaves brought around plates of dessert, she slipped a dainty foot free of her red stiletto. Slipping it between the captain's knees, where one slim ankle made to caress the inside of this thigh.

It was too much.

Without much warning at all, nausea bubbled up the back of my throat. My distress going utterly unnoticed in the face of Carina's sickly-sweet charm.

Ribs heaving with force enough to crack bone, I vomited. Expelling my steak dinner in a gush of vile chunks all over Carina's pretty red heels.

It filled the empty shoe, splashed between her toes when she recoiled with a caw of shock. And then, when she launched herself back from the table, she slipped in the warm, slick bile—launching her shin straight into the cross beam supporting the table legs with a *thunk* that clattered silverware and made glass dance.

Outraged, in pain, Carina shrieked her horror. Her eyes bulging from that beautiful, flushed face. An uneven limp sending her careening away from the table when the reality of what I'd done began to sink in.

"You disgusting little bitch!" she screamed, hands clenched at her sides. Gait uneven as she pranced in place. A bruise already blooming on her shin.

I wiped the back of my mouth, watching her without daring to blink. Braced for the strike.

"Fucksakes, Mila," the captain hissed, and drew me to my feet. Offering a serviette in one hand, another glass of water in the other. "Are you alright?"

I shrugged, eyes following Carina as a flock of slaves fluttered around her. Cleaning and primping. "I tried to tell you," I whispered, humiliated despite how much better I felt. My stomach relieved, my system flushed with adrenaline.

The captain snorted. "Yes," he said. "I suppose you did."

"Well," the general said, then stood. Chair scraping on the polished tile floor, he folded his serviette with careful, precise movements, and said, "Seems to be a reasonable place to call an end to the festivities. Captain Rawlings," he added, voice thick with the ring of authority, "I expect to see you at headquarters for an assessment of your newfound power. Bright and early."

"Sir." The captain's jaw flexed at the corner, his chin dipping in a tight nod, he took the back of my neck in the palm of his hand. Fingers almost touching where my throat worked around a tense swallow. "My apologies," he said, addressing the gathered elites with a tense little smile. "It seems it's not so simple to take the wildcat out of the forest, after all."

I blushed, chased from the dining hall from another round of condescending male laughter. My nape soaked through with humiliation as the captain drove me from the general's manse. Where the last of Tritan's priestesses knelt in supplication, unable to so much as lift their eyes, their fires were banked with a thick layer of frost.

Strides long and sure, the captain gave me no

chance to collect myself until we were well away from the suffocating fog of stolen elite power.

But there, beneath it all, I was flushed with an odd sense of victory. For despite everything—the threats and the lurking, ever-present danger—I had managed to do something profound, no matter how disgusting.

A slimy, chunky victory, but a victory nevertheless.

4

———————

I took a breath of fresh evening air, a tiny smile spreading across my lips, for with every step, General Tilcot's stolen manse grew smaller. His threats and lingering glances a problem for another day, as the stink of elites was washed from my sinuses.

All except one.

The very worst—the one I couldn't escape.

"Mila." Fingers bracketing either side of my throat, the captain took the back of my neck in his rough palm. A possessive collar stiff with the simmering promise of violence. His shoulders still rigid, despite the distance his long-legged strides put between us and the manse.

I tried to shake him off and failed.

"Feeling brave again, I see," the captain drawled, but his grip only tightened.

"And why not?" I replied, flush with a newfound arrogance and adrenaline. "You've lost your leverage, *Asher*. And until I find a way to free my people, I take solace in knowing that pig of a general won't kill the Head Priestess."

Tension rippled through him, into me. A tight, "Is that so?" said in an aristocratic purr the only indication of the nerve I'd struck. The weakness I'd found that might be exploited.

"You're parasites," I added as we rounded a corner and the captain's residence came into view, clinging to what remained of the confidence I'd found in ruining Carina's pretty shoes. "And without a host, the parasite is nothing. It's *you* who need *us*."

The captain said nothing. Made no effort to interject and showed no reaction, except for the bulging muscle twitching at the corner of his jaw. It wasn't until he'd driven us through the front door of his townhouse that I felt a tingle in my wrists and throat—the only warning of the captain's influence surging in my veins before I was held immobile.

"Have you forgotten?" he said, and pressed my pliant body against the nearest wall, kicking the door closed with a snap. "I don't need leverage to bend you to my will." Heated breath traced the shell of my ear, his head dipping low so full lips might brush my skin. So the rasp of teeth could leave my skin scored with a trail of reddened gooseflesh in their wake.

I swallowed, trembling in his shadow, but that

was all. Held still, unable to speak with my jaws sealed shut.

"Even before you were mine," he murmured, and let his fingers trail down my throat. Over each bump of my windpipe, before he paused to trace the hollow between my collar bones. "*Irrevocably* mine…" Rough hands slipped down, traced the crease between my breasts, then found purchase beneath. Thumbs and forefingers teasing the underside of my breasts, he squeezed my ribs and trapped my breath in a tight band of compression that made me feel grounded and untethered all at once. And then, through a smirk, he whispered, "You were made to kneel, Mila."

With the fuse on my temper lit, his influence faded away, leaving me free to hurl, "Is that so?" back in his face, but with only half the sinister intention.

A smile flicked against the edge of my jaw, just beneath my ear. Drawing up a cascading wave of shivers that pimpled my nape. My scalp. "Mmhmm. No matter how hard you fight to deny it," he hummed, and drove me back with his hands still tight around my ribs, "it's where you long to be."

Despite everything—the press of his body against mine, the humiliation and anguish, the loss of all control—I laughed. "I long to see the empire fall. To see—"

His fingertips trailed along the skin peeking above my waist, at the base of my spine where I was bare and vulnerable. A ticklish invasion that saw me lurch away from his touch, our hips bumping together.

A dark smile lit his features, but I pressed on, forcing my words through clenched and pointed teeth. "I long to see every filthy Caledonian parasite brought low. Everything you've stolen returned and made whole."

He hummed, pressing his lips to my temple, and said, "Because you're a little ball of fire, Mila." At the press of his thickly muscled thigh between my legs, I gasped. Tried to buck his influence and failed. "All fire and fury," he said, stroking the delicate skin of my throat. "Just begging to be tamed."

"Even if that were true," I said as he dipped his head to lick my collarbone, a lock of his silky black hair teasing the underside of my jaw, my cheek, "it will *never* be you."

"Mmm, yes, you hate me," he said in a voice that sent wicked amusement rumbling through my chest.

My reply rolled off my tongue without an instant of hesitation. "With every fiber of my being."

He straightened, all sharp angles and hard lines. A predator closing on the kill. "And that, my dear Mila, is the most passionate emotion of them all," he whispered, and, lips moving against my ear, he cupped my bottom. Spread my cheeks and pulled my core against his thigh before bending at the knee. He lifted me, left me to ride his thigh while his hands remained free to roam. "It'll take nothing to flip that coin and turn your hatred into devotion." Making a fist in the hair at my nape, he angled my head back. Exposing my throat to his lips and teeth. "It's a challenge I relish. One *you* are unequal to, priestess."

Voice breaking, I said, "Don't touch me."

"Frightened?" he murmured, lips tracing my thrashing pulse.

"Nauseated," I snapped, trying not to squirm. My feet dangling, body useless. Disobedient to my silent commands.

At that, he withdrew with a devious chuckle. Issuing a pithy *tsk* as he said, "Mmm. Then I know just what you need."

"Oh? Like I need a good steak, Asher?"

"And that," he said in a deadly whisper, "is the third time you've used my name. A privilege I have not granted you."

A chill spilled down my back. "So it's to be another whipping then?" I asked, voice trembling despite the nerve I'd struck. Because of it.

"No, my beautiful, wild pet." He kissed the shell of my ear. "I'm going to fuck you on every piece of furniture in this house. Show you what it means to be a priestess bound to an elite."

But before I could respond, he hiked my skirts, jerked me away from the wall, and spun me. Giving me barely enough time to get my feet beneath me before he had me bent over a hall-stand topped with a vase full of drooping, cut flowers.

I gasped, scrambling for purchase and sent the vase flying with a careless backhand. An instant later, the small desperate noises he'd torn from my throat were swallowed up by the sounds of shattering glass.

The full weight of an aroused, Caledonian elite fell across my back. Pinning me more effectively than even his influence might, and at my ear, he breathed a husky, "That was my favorite vase, Mila."

Squirming, I tried to drag a breath through clenched teeth—and my eyes caught on the edge of an ornate picture frame. "And I suppose this is your favorite painting?" I snarled, and tore it from the wall in a shower of paint chips and dust.

A heavy hand fell between my shoulder blades, forcing me flat. His grin spreading across my nape, where his lips teased. "Nothing more than trashy Eloran art, pet." At this, both of his hands slid down my back. He found purchase around my ribs once more, before they slipped forward. Beneath the flimsy illusion of modesty that was my silk dressing, he took liberties that stole my breath.

Cupping my breasts, squeezing the fat, he pinched my nipples between forefinger and thumb, rolling until he drew the points into tight little beads of aching tension. Before he released me and shoved my dress clear, both sides pushed down and forward. The material gathered in a single fist that rested in a rope between my breasts, his fist bunched in the hollow spot where my ribs met my sternum. My breasts hanging free, nipples grazing the chill wood of the tabletop beneath me.

But it was his free hand that made me whine, terror and something without name lodged high at the back of my throat. "Wait, *please*—"

His grip landed on my right hip. Fingers clenching hard enough to bruise, the captain pressed his nose into my hair and drew in a ragged breath. And on his exhale, a raspy, "*Intoxicating*," ruffled the fine hairs shielding my ear, leaving me coated in a layer of gooseflesh and shame.

Straining for breath, for sanctuary, I shouted a desperate, "I have diseases!" in a voice that tasted of splintered glass.

His hand trailed down my hip, twisting in the fluttery loose fabric that kissed my ankles. Drawing it up, higher with every bunching twist. "Mmm. What kind of diseases, pet?"

Choking on an anguished sob, I whispered, "The sexual kind."

The puff of a sinister chuckle kissed the back of my neck. "*Very* convincing." And, kicking my ankles apart, he exposed the flesh at the top of my thighs. Leaving a heap of fabric bunched on the shelf of my bottom, where I was bent and vulnerable. Laid bare, when a moment later, the captain wrenched the last of my dress clear. Leaving me exposed to the evening chill. Unwrapped only enough to suit his lewd intentions.

One fist anchoring me to the hall-stand, he leaned back and I felt the heat of that obsidian glare ravaging my most intimate parts. "Such beauty," he cooed as his fingers trailed over the curve of my hip. Thumb hooking the right cheek of my bottom, he spread me. Groaning at what he saw. "It's a wonder you managed to evade us for so long."

Wheezing, I squeezed my eyes shut and heard the ominous whirr of a zipper.

And then I knew.

He was right.

It didn't matter how hard I fought, the strength of my logic, nor how valiantly I might struggle— Captain Asher Rawlings could simply take whatever he wanted. With nothing but an errant thought, he had my submission. The dark flames of poisonous elite energy an infection that spread through my veins and left me too hot. Flesh aching with alien need, despite the way my heart thrashed at the back of my throat, the organ panicked and trying to escape. To spare me this final horror.

"Please," I breathed, and felt something blunt press against my core. Making me throb. Clench. "Please, *don't*—"

"I can feel it, Mila," he rasped, and leaned back. Releasing the fabric at my front, he left my breasts swinging free and claimed one cheek of my bottom in either hand. Peeled me apart so he might have an unobstructed view at the thing he meant to ruin.

"Your fear." Thumbs sliding in tandem, he caught the lips of my sex and made them gape around what was blunt and foreign. "The intoxicating sweetness of your helpless curiosity. The way you ache..." I felt his hips shift, the burning stretch of secret flesh yielding to a force greater than any I'd ever dared imagine. "I'm already inside you, and I can feel it all. That's how I know—you were born to serve an elite," he whispered, not unaffected by the weight of this moment. Poised at my entrance, hanging on the edge of something unforgivable as if to savor what I'd never willingly give.

The front door banged open.

Startled, the captain's hips sluiced forward a fraction of an inch, making me hiss in shock. Frozen by his influence, my breasts rippling with the tension snapping taut between us both. Every inch of my flesh on full, lewd display to an intruder I couldn't see.

"Holy shit, captain," came a voice I recognized, but couldn't place. "Sorry, sir. I didn't mean—"

"What are you doing here, Marco," the captain drawled, unhurried, despite the strain I could feel vibrating through his muscle. "And why," he added, and stroked the length of my spine with the flat of one hand, "can't it wait for morning?"

"The rebels are attacking, sir." Marco cleared his throat, not totally able to mask the edge of excitement when he said, "They've got something *new*. And

General Tilcot wants you on the frontlines to test out the new girl. Now."

"She hasn't even been assessed yet," the captain spat, pushing just a little more of himself through the slick ache of swollen lips.

Marco chuckled. "Tilcot said he'd bring Sasha so, and this is a direct quote, mind, 'You have nothing to worry about, boy.'"

At this, the captain huffed a deep, frustrated sigh and let my dress fall. "Insufferable prick." Shifting forward, he adjusted my front and hid my breasts from view before tucking himself away.

Released from his compulsion, I sank to the floor amid the shards of broken glass and plaster. My breath hitching, cheeks wet. Back pressed to the wall where I cowered and shook with relief. Adrenaline burning in my veins.

"Come along, priestess," the captain said, extending his hand—the very same extremity I could still feel on my hip. On my chest and in the lingering ache throbbing between my thighs. "Let's test out my new power."

I shook my head, teeth bared. Confidence in tatters, but still, a defiant, "No," rolled off my tongue with spiteful ease.

"Wasn't a question, Mila," he replied as Marco handed him a jacket.

"You know... we could always stay," Marco said, eyebrows waggling. A lewd grin spread across his lips to reveal slightly crooked teeth. "Just for a little while. Wouldn't mind a free show…"

Hissing, I scrambled to my feet in a rush that left me dizzy. Swaying without daring to tear my scowl from Marco's face, I opted for open conflict between warring nations over a private show. "I'd prefer death."

Marco clutched at his chest as if wounded, and the captain reclaimed his grip on my nape, pressed his lips into my hair, and said, "How easy the coin turns."

5

The front lines.

I shivered as a roiling wave of nausea came over me. Stinging where a now distinct sort of pressure weighed heavy at the back of my throat—a threat that meant to strangle before it bubbled over. To reject the very thought that I would be used to slaughter rebels. My power turned against the people I'd sacrificed so much to save.

"*Please*," I whispered, setting my heels as he threw open the front door, one hand wrapped firmly about my wrist. "Don't do this."

Inky eyes flicked back for an instant before he snorted.

I swallowed, throwing my weight back. Toward the chips of plaster and broken glass where the captain had almost had his way and taken everything

I'd never give. "We're healers," I whispered, frantic and flailing for rescue. "Not murderers."

"No," he replied, and ushered me into the evening breeze once more. "You're slaves. Tools of war owned by the empire." He locked the door, fingers never leaving my wrist. "It's time you learn what it really means to be a priestess."

"You can't—"

A tingle surged to life in my wrists and throat, and without so much as bothering to glance back, he showed me that yes, in fact, he *could*.

In the street in front of the captain's townhouse, a utilitarian, battered coach sat idling by the curb. No hint of gaudy decoration. Not a glimmer of obnoxious Caledonian pomp, it was a vehicle meant to ferry soldiers.

Nothing more.

Surging forward on long legs, Marco claimed a seat behind the wheel. "Come on," he said, and flicked a lighter with his left thumb, igniting a cigarette in a puff of sweet smoke. The cherry glowed a bright, cheerful shade of red before he exhaled. "You're gonna want to see this, sir."

"Dare I trust you behind the wheel?" the captain drawled, jaw tight when he opened the door and ushered me inside, giving me no room to fight him. Almost as if the great and powerful Captain Rawlings were hesitant to give up an inch of control.

"See," Marco said, and shifted the coach into gear,

"it's this kind of flagrant disrespect that really erodes the confidence of the men, sir."

Hurling down the cobbled streets, Marco sent the vehicle lurching to the left, narrowly avoiding a collision with another parked coach before careening around a sharp corner carrying too much speed.

"We need *encouragement*," Marco said, dragging the word out as the coach picked up a nauseating velocity. Buildings and pedestrians zipping by at an ever greater pace. "A leader who builds confidence and rewards the skills of his men"—he jerked the wheel and sent us into a fishtail around another sharp right turn—"with incentives. Like access to high-quality pussy. All expenses paid. Vacations that last longer than a night off at the bathhouse."

Knuckles white, I clung to the door handle and slid into the captain's hip, a gasp of shocked terror caught high at the back of my throat.

"Fucksakes, Marco," the captain hissed, and dragged me off the bench and into his lap. "Slow down or the only pussy you'll see for the next year is the one between your own cheeks. You'll have to find a mirror and bend to see it."

Marco gasped, his attention leaving the cobbled streets as he spun to stare at the captain in open-mouthed shock. "You wouldn't dare!"

The only response offered was a tight jaw an unblinking glare.

With a huff, Marco flicked the last half of his

smoke out the window where it flew by in a shower of sparks, steering one-handed as he took another aggressive corner and sent the captain and I rocketing toward the opposite door. "We're almost there, you old prude. And just for the record," he grumbled, "you'd be lost without me."

Taking a deep breath, the captain reached with his left hand and wrapped white knuckles around a handle hanging from the roof. Enveloping me in his scent, he anchored me to his lap, pressed his lips to my ear, and murmured, "Just close your eyes, pet. Deep breaths."

And for the first time, I didn't fight for space. Didn't argue or bicker. Heart in throat, a visceral fear for my life pulsed behind my eyes. Writhing as if it were a living thing that sent vicious, icy cold barbs spiking into my heart and racing down the inside of my spine, leaving my hands to tingle. My toes numb where they were braced against plush carpet, feet tangled between the captain's.

"Annnd"—Marco threw the vehicle into park —"that's a new base record, lady and gent!"

Staggering from the coach, the captain hauled me out. Fingers too tight where they were wrapped around my elbow, his face sallow and tinged just the slightest shade of green—a sentiment surely reflected on my own face.

Before either of us could cherish the relief, the captain was surrounded by solders. Swamped with a deluge of information and questions. And, sending one last scathing glare over his shoulder at Marco, he silenced them all with a raised hand, and said, "What's the situation, Gabe?"

"They've built a shield, sir," the soldier said. "Our weapons don't have enough firepower to punch through them." Gabe patted a matte black weapon strapped to his hip with a grimace. "Hoping an elite can get the job done where we can't, or we've got some serious problems. General Tilcot wants it to be you, sir."

I jerked as if slapped. Eyes flicking between the captain and Gabe, impending murder forgotten in the face of this new information. This sneak peek behind enemy lines, for everything I'd heard over my years of battling the empire, it had been my assumption that only an elite could use an energy weapon.

None of the slavers I'd come across had access to such a thing, but if the soldiers of the Caledonian army did?

The Elorans had already lost this war, no matter what kind of technology they managed to forge in the depths of their exile.

But... if the Caledonians had managed to give their regular soldiers the power of an elite, unfettered access to their devastating weaponry... perhaps there was a glaring opportunity for me to do the same...

Long legs propelling him up a set of rickety stairs and into a shoddy, makeshift building, the captain hauled me along in his wake without saying a word. Without touching me, he held me in thrall. His influence a gentle pulse of pins that pierced my veins midway up my forearms. Wrists and throat tingling, he kept me utterly enslaved as he approached a large glass case in the center of a room packed with soldiers. Running his fingers along the edge of a sealed lid, he paused to caress a bronze latch. Eyes going bottomless and inky with the same gleam I'd seen only minutes before.

Lust.

I could name it, now. Recognized the thing that burned and left me with scars I could only feel. Couldn't see.

He flicked the latch.

Silence fell on the gathered soldiers. A hush that drew my nape tight with the sort of tension that spoke of something deadly lurking in the wood. That I'd stumbled into the den of a predator more vicious than any I'd ever known before.

Reverent, he put hands on the massive, cruel thing inside.

A cannon twice the length of my forearm, three times as thick. Matte black with chrome accents marking levers and knobs.

At the first instant of contact, it came to life with an angry series of beeps. The muzzle glowed the most intense, vibrant shade of green I'd ever seen. Enough that it made me hiss and recoil, overshadowing the burn of my manacles—now creeping past my elbows in a slow, agonizing burn—but only for an instant.

The men cheered.

"*Shiiit*, sir," Marco said, and slapped the captain's back. "Looks like the wildcat packs a helluva punch!"

Grinning, the captain merely caught my eye. Watching as I tried to rub. Tried to push the golden burn back down into the manacles from which it had come. That sinister glimmer swirling in his eyes growing all the more ravenous the longer he looked.

"Never seen a weapon charge so quickly," Gabe said, a distinct note of awe in his voice.

"Owning a priestess does have its advantages," the captain drawled, and stroked the side of my face with his free hand. Balancing an instrument of mass destruction on his hip. "Now," he said, "let's see what we can do about these rebels and their shields, shall we?" He placed a hand on my back, once more guiding me from the building into the cool evening air.

And though I couldn't feel much else with the power that had been stolen from me, I could feel the undeniable bubble of excitement just waiting to boil over.

The *captain's* elation at the prospect of bloodshed.

I tripped, staggering along at his side. "What are you going to do?" I asked, voice a pathetic quiver that held no strength as I tried to right myself.

He steadied me. "Whatever needs to be done."

"It would seem," Gabe said, easily matching the captain's pace, "their shields are absorbing the energy from our weapons before we can even come close to punching through. Dispersing it, maybe, I'm not sure yet. What I'd really need," he added, and flipped through a folder with a scowl, "is to study one before it's destroyed. But we ran out of charge cells half an hour ago, and the rebels have been advancing ever since."

"Clever bastards," the captain murmured, adjusting the cannon where it sat on his hip. "Marco, order a new shipment of cells and inform General Tilcot of this development."

"Already done, sir," Marco said with a smug smile. "And the general is on the way. Said he'd like to see this for himself."

From the corner of my eye, I watched the captain's lip curl, and I was the only one who heard him say, "I'll just bet he does." And louder, "It's hard to imagine they could've come up with a viable defense," he said, and turned dark eyes down. Idly checking the mechanisms of his cannon, avoiding eye contact as he busied himself with the menial task. "In the meantime, allow me to charge your cells, gentlemen."

Both soldiers removed chunky black boxes from their weapons and handed them over without complaint or hesitation. Almost eager as they watched.

Just as it had with the cannon, the internal features of the cells lit up the instant it touched the captain's skin. An intense, glowing green I could see through my lids no matter how hard I squeezed my eyes shut.

And the burn.

It burrowed deeper. Sinking beneath my skin and into the bone where it charred my meat. Passing my elbows in a brief flare, before it receded back to simmer in my wrists. My throat.

The captain's bark of laughter surprised me, but when he tossed the charge cells back to his soldiers and spun, scooping me up in his arms, I gasped. Stupefied when he bent to claim my lips in a searing, blatant display of ownership that was met with jeers of encouragement from the gathered soldiers. "The things I'm going to do with you," he murmured, and flexed. Making me feel the bulge of angry possession where it was trapped behind his slacks. Throbbing, held barely in check. And then, louder, so his men might hear, "Rebel scum aren't going to know what's hit them, boys!"

The men cheered.

But my blood ran cold.

Clotted and thick in my veins, for although I could feel a whisper of the captain's eager glee, I couldn't help the way my eyes strayed. Pulse pounding high at the back of my throat, I searched the horizon for the rebels. The Elorans who would die by my hand, because of the man who'd claimed me for the empire. A man who meant to use my power for murder.

"We'd better stop here, sir," Gabe said when we reached the crumbling, burnt-out shell of what might have once been a park. Crouching behind a low wall, he added, "Don't want to give them the advantage in this half-light."

"How close are they?" the captain asked in an undertone, scanning the area.

Gabe jerked the muzzle of his weapon. "Few hundred meters north, sir. Just past that statue. Got the rest of the unit waiting behind those buildings with the last of our charge cells. Ready to flank 'em if they're stupid enough to make another push forward," he said, nodding to the abandoned houses behind us.

"Perfect," the captain said, and without warning, went utterly stiff. His shoulders rigid, tension building in every line of his frame.

Startled by the sudden change, I tried to taste that pillar of elite power. Tried to see through his eyes and found nothing but what he'd left anchored in my blood and sinew. My senses blind to all but Captain Asher Rawlings.

The crunch of heavy, approaching boots made

me jump and I spun just in time to see a face I hated before he spoke.

"Gentlemen," General Tilcot said, leering as he glared down the length of his nose. Eyes fixed to me when he too knelt behind the crumbling shelf of ruined concrete.

"Come for the show?" the captain asked without taking his eyes off the field.

But I heard nothing else of their whispered rivalry, for the creature skulking in the general's wake claimed every forgotten ounce of my attention.

The Head Priestess.

Consumed in the general's shadow, she was a shell of the woman I'd been taught to fear. No longer the leader of the temple my father had hidden me from since the day my status as a priestess had begun to manifest.

Instead, her head was bowed. Eyes downcast, her shoulders slumped and curled, protective of what little she had left. Whatever spark remained that kept breath moving in her chest.

Broken.

The word echoed through my skull. A perfect description of the creature I couldn't bring myself to look away from.

"Are..." I swallowed. Wet my throat and tried again. "Are you okay?" I whispered, and heard nothing of the men discussing strategies to subdue the rebels. My gaze fixed to the sallow, empty face before me.

She flinched, but that was all.

"I'm sorry," I pressed, knowing it wasn't enough. It would never be enough... wasn't so much as a start.

But when she turned liquid blue eyes up, blinking as the ghost of an understanding smile lit her pale face, I knew it was... *something.*

"Quit your stalling, Asher," the general said and broke the spell. "We need a prisoner or two for the inauguration of the new elites." A smug little smirk tugged at the edge of his lips. "I've managed to entice the capitol this year, which means we might just have ourselves a royal visit. Let's see what you can do with our wildcat."

"She's *my* wildcat, sir," the captain retorted beneath his breath. Irritated and sulking, but to Marco, he said, "Take her to cover, but make sure she's got a good view."

Marco's grip landed on my shoulder. "With pleasure, sir."

I slapped his hand away, set my teeth, and said, "I won't let you do this."

The captain blinked. Tearing his gaze from the field, he turned to face me with a slow roll of his neck. A viper's smile drawn tight across his lips. "Is that so? Tell me, priestess," he drawled, and sent the full might of his power pounding through my veins. Making me smolder from the inside out, skin searing with the burn of submission that lit my very blood ablaze. And then he forced me to my knees before an audience of men who devoured every instant of the confrontation, and said, "How exactly do you plan to stop me? And please..." He paused, extended one finger to trace a line between my breasts. "Be explicit."

Scowling, I refused to blink, trying with all my might to fight his influence. To ignore the trail of blazing flesh left in his wake and gain some equal standing.

The lick of dark flames stroked at the backside of my ribs, the captain filling me from the inside. Making sure I felt it when he rose to the unspoken challenge. That I was with him when his head tipped to one side, tongue darting out to wet his lips...

... *when he forced me to bow.*

His point made, the weight of his influence evaporated. Leaving me gasping and trembling where I'd been submitted in the dirt. On my knees. Unable to find the courage to lift my head and see the gloating, Caledonian smirks I knew were weighing me down.

Strong fingers wrapped around my elbow and the captain drew me to my feet. Pressing my cheek to his chest so I might hear the heavy thump of a heart I wished would stop beating. "It'll get easier," he murmured, tangling his fingers in a sheet of silky, silver-blonde hair just to tug my head back. To force our eyes to meet. "Accepting your place at my feet."

He smoothed my hair back, clearing my forehead before his thumb dropped to trace the ridge of my left cheekbone. "As mine."

A hiccup spilled over my lips, voice strained and fragile, but still, I said, "No," with all the hatred I could muster.

He grinned, showing teeth. "Fire and fury, Mila," he whispered, reminding me of his threat to turn a coin. He spun me then, sending me stumbling into Marco's arms and said, "To the barracks with a view, if you please."

Marco engaged his weapon and tapped the muzzle to his brow. "Yes, sir."

"Sasha, you too," the general said, and flicked his wrist at the Head Priestess, dismissing her. Watching me with murky eyes.

With a shiver, I turned away. Not willing to test the captain where the general might be motivated to assume my punishment.

Cool, dry fingers slipped between mine, unwinding my clenched fist.

It was the Head Priestess. Her touch soothing to the inferno of tempered flames. The helpless, seething mass of hatred I couldn't act upon calmed by her offer of... something.

A thing only another priestess might understand, for we were to be made to watch the murder of innocents. Made to participate.

To watch, and know the blood spilled was blood

we'd be forced to wear into the Void between this life and the next.

Marco guided us to the shoddy headquarters building, holding the door as if a Caledonian soldier had any idea what it was to be a gentleman. "By the windows," he said, and pulled the Head Priestess' chair out, offering an upturned palm as she perched on the ledge of a three-legged stool and set sightless eyes to the pockmarked wreckage before us.

A sight she'd seen often enough not to be alarmed by it. Desensitized by the carnage.

I cleared my throat, ignoring the wave of numb terror washing over my skin. "Baby-sitting duty suits you," I snipped, and crossed my arms over my breasts. Jaw clenched, manacles stuffed out of sight. Into my armpits.

Marco lit another cigarette, took a drag, and mirrored my posture. Bumping one hip against the counter, his back to the row of windows as he watched me. Amusement flickering across his face. "Wouldn't call it that," he said at length, exhaling a cloud of sweet smoke in a jet toward the ceiling.

I sneered. "What else could it possibly be? You're in here, made to watch with the *slaves*," I spat, "while the menfolk do the killing."

"Or," Marco returned, and let me see the flash of slightly crooked teeth, "Captain Rawlings has assigned his best soldier to safe-guard his most valuable asset in a less than ideal situation."

I whirled to face him, clenched fists held stiff at my sides. "That man cares *nothing* for my safety," I hissed, fury spattering between the points of my modified canines. "He isn't capable of it."

Marco shrugged. "Not sure the distinction matters all that much."

"And why would it?" I asked, a bark of bitter laughter bursting free of my lips. "Nothing matters as long as the empire has access to their precious assets, is that it?"

Taking another deep drag, the soldier's smirk became a grin. "Now you're getting it." A tendril of smoke curled from his nostrils before he snorted, and said, "Not sure what you've got to complain about, lady wildcat. You were rescued from a life of struggle and starvation, living in the forest with nothing and no one. And now?" His hands flew out, an all-encompassing gesture that swallowed our surroundings. "Luxury, food, and security in exchange for power your people couldn't even use without an elite to harvest it."

Shock rendered me mute. My lips working around a stupefied silence. That this soldier thought so little of the women who'd been stolen from a life of peace and altruism? Women who'd been made to kill for a country that wasn't their own, whose power of healing had been so corrupted by warmongers.

Caledonian propaganda. Indoctrination for evils

the average citizen hadn't thought to ask forgiveness for.

"That's"—I shook my head, rubbing at the burn in my throat as I searched for a rebuttal, and failed.

But a moment later, the burn became something else. A reminder of what it had felt like when the chains were first bound to my skin, when I'd lost everything at the captain's hands. Incinerating heat that didn't scorch looped around my throat and wrists, the glow from my Tritan chains lit up Marco's face.

I couldn't even scream. Couldn't only gape at Marco's awed, slack-jawed expression and know my veins were bulging with molten fire that had traveled up, over my forearms, past my elbows on its way to cauterize my heart and wrap it in a beautiful, inert cast of pure gold.

"Such power," Marco whispered, and turned to watch the window. "Come, lady wildcat. This is what you were meant for."

But I couldn't move. Paralyzed in a tomb of complete agony, my lungs seized solid and immobile as the gold crept and wormed. Crackling beneath my skin, baking my flesh.

And then three things happened all at once.

Pure, unfiltered torment tore through my chest— and was gone in an instant, leaving me utterly boneless. Drained to the point of collapse.

A flash of blinding green ignited the distant field,

imprinting the contents of the headquarters building into my retinas as the world tilted back on its axis.

My knees kissed the floor, unnoticed in the wake of a mighty explosion.

"Holy shit!" Marco hollered, whopping along with the rest of the soldiers packed into the safety of the headquarters building. "That was incredible! Lady wildcat, you're—"

But that was all I knew before the last speck of light faded from my vision and everything fell into darkness.

6
___

"**M**arco, you have to stop him!"

The voice echoed from a long way off. Familiar and alien all at once. Distorted through the heavy, wet sands clogging my ears. Each wave of sound pulling me deeper beneath the surface where it was quiet. Where I might stay forever.

"He's killing her! *Hurry!*"

A muffled curse fizzled against my ears, and the tingling between my eyes spread to the bridge of my nose. My lips and cheeks. Spilling down my chest, where it seeped into numb extremities, leaving my heart to flounder and skip in an irregular beat.

"Mila!" the voice sobbed, and I felt a tendril of something warm and beautiful press against my cheeks. A slight compression that puckered my lips.

The cold swallowed it whole and reached for

more with a sucking, ravenous greed. Pulling with such ferocious demand that a tiny, fragile sound of protest slipped through my lips.

A gasp, and the beauty was taken away. "I can't fix this, Marco! Run! You have to stop him before—"

The voice faded into the frost. Replaced by the electric tingle, a coating of falling dust that was heavier than anything I might lift alone.

And why bother?

This was a place without pain. Without anguish or torment, where I couldn't be used to kill the people I'd die to save. A place without grief, where my breaths were rigid and frozen in my chest, but only for a moment. Only until the cold began to feel like heat, and the prickle of withering nerves became the searing burn of... life.

A tiny, fragile flicker ignited in my chest as the gushing exodus of my life-force came to an abrupt, merciful halt.

My eyes flicked open an instant before a breath was forced through my lips and into my lungs. Warmed by lips that weren't my own.

Silver-blonde hair.

Tearful blue eyes rimmed in red that shimmered when they focused on mine.

And just there, crinkled at the corner of those eyes, the gentle whisper of age.

"Oh, Goddess, Mila," the Head Priestess whispered, cradling my face between her palms. "Breath for me, girl. That's it. Another deep breath, all the way to the bottom. Just one more."

Ribs screaming a wordless protest, I did as she bade despite the wet wheeze that crackled in my lungs. "What—" I coughed, weak and helpless where I was cradled in her lap. "What happened?"

She swallowed, tearing her gaze away as if in search of the words. And then, "I think..." She smoothed her palms over my sternum. Fidgeting with the rumpled edges of my silken dress. "Mila... I think you're a—"

But before she could tell me what I was, a mighty crash shook the entire building.

The captain burst through the door with frantic chaos gleaming in eyes gone deep as pitch. "Where is she!?" he bellowed, pausing only long enough to seek out my limp form before he was moving in a rush. Sinking to his knees, he scooped gentle hands beneath my thighs, cradled my head, and pulled my pliant body into his embrace.

And without saying a word, without bothering himself to ask what had happened, he filled me with the kiss of dark flames. Elite energy pulsed to life in the place where my senses had once been saturated with *my* natural gifts. Licking at every forgotten corner, his attention seeped through the places that hurt and left them aching with something far, *far* worse than desiccation and rot.

"Stop." I pushed at his hands, voice a hoarse whisper of helpless denial.

"Don't move," he barked, brow furrowed as if in great concentration to utilize a skill he should not possess. Assessing my health for himself with the rightful power of a *priestess*.

I flashed my teeth, and though I fell limp against the heat of his chest—luxuriating in ecstasy of elite energy replacing what had been sucked away—I mustered a scathing, "Don't tell me what to do."

A breathless chuckle was pressed against my temple, lips daring to press a smile into sweat-damp skin as his fingers found their way into my hair and stroked at my scalp. "Glad to see your mouth's intact."

"Sasha," General Tilcot snapped, the next to fill my bleary line of sight as he loomed above us. "What happened?"

The Head Priestess wrung her hands where they were folded in her lap. Eyes downcast, a sheen of anxious sweat glistening on her brow. "The girl"— she cleared her throat—"she hasn't been trained, sir. I would have noticed if I'd had the chance to test her—"

Stomping forward, the general seized a handful of the Head Priestess' hair and hauled her up. "Don't be fucking coy, Sasha. Explain this. *Now.*"

Both hands wrapped about his wrist, she writhed in place, but said, "She's not a priestess, sir! Please!"

Going still, the captain's grip grew tight where he cradled me against him. Possessive and stiff.

An ugly bark of laughter burst from the general's lips. "What I just saw on the field would beg to differ. Try again," he cooed, and hauled back on her scalp. Making the Head Priestess arch into his thigh. Exposing herself to the cruel whims of a monster, showing complete submission in a bared and exposed throat.

But despite the tears, she said, "She isn't, sir. Not really." She gasped as long, cruel fingers wrapped about her throat and squeezed. "Mila was never trained in the temple! Her power is volatile—*please,* sir!" she begged, standing at the very point of her toes to relieve the pressure on her scalp. "The girl is dangerous. To herself and Captain Rawlings."

Murky eyes pinched with suspicion, the general said, "Go on."

"She's an empath—the very thing we strive to avoid and the reason the temple seeks to take in fledgling priestesses. I don't know how it might have happened, but her power was left to mature unchecked, festering when it should have been guided. Nurtured." A tattered, pained sob spilled over the Head Priestess' lips, but she pressed on. "Instead of being centered inside, where it can be throttled and protected, her energy is tied to everything around her. She's n-never learned to separate herself from it."

"Sounds like she's a bottomless resource to me," the general said, and released his grip on her throat, smoothing his fingers over the red marks he'd left behind.

But the Head Priestess shook her head. "Her life force is tangled too deep. If you fire your weapon," she said, and caught the captain's eye, "you'll drain her long before you can exhaust the energy she's tied to. You'll kill her, like you almost did tonight."

For a moment, silence reigned in the headquarters building. Heavy and oppressive, for deep in the center of my heart, where the memory of my father lived to whisper warnings and advice, I knew she was right.

That I'd been sheltered and spoiled did not come as a shock. But to learn that one misinformed decision—what might have been my doom—was the one thing that offered a glimmer of salvation?

I laughed. Saturated in elite energy, surrounded by the distant sounds of ongoing battle, I began to shake with the sort of mirth born from exhaustion and peak irony. "You can't use your new toy without breaking it," I gasped, head lolling where it hung over the captain's bicep. Mocking him in a room packed with his peers.

The general let go his hold on the Head Priestess' scalp, and turned that murky scowl upon me. "Can she be trained?" he barked, fists clenching at his sides. As if aching to wrap around *my* throat and squeeze... "Trained to use this... this empath power for the empire?"

Rubbing at the place where cruel fingerprints bruised her skin, the Head Priestess' shoulders hunched. "I-I don't know," she stammered. "It's never been done before."

"The fuck do you mean, '*It's never been done?*'" Tilcot snarled, whirling to face her once more. "Were you, or were you not the leader of these simpering bitches?"

She took a step back. "I-I was," she said. "But you don't understand, sir, an empath is—"

"An incomparable asset to the empire and one I intend to utilize. One the royal family is going to want to see in action themselves."

Blinking, the Head Priestess ignored his interruption, and said, "They're incredibly rare. The last one was centuries before my time." Carefully avoiding my eye, she fidgeted with the fabric swirling about her knees for a moment before continuing. "But we have to try. It's too dangerous to leave her like this, surrounded by elites. All this energy—her symptoms will only get worse."

"Very good," the general said, and straightened to his full height. "Until then, Rawlings, you're off active duty."

Fingers growing painfully tight, the captain swallowed his protest.

I felt it. In the way his temper flared with seething

contempt, the dark flames lashing out behind my ribs as if his ire were my own.

But he held his silence and crushed me to his chest.

"Have your men clean run cleanup for the mess you made," the general added. "I want that shield in empire hands before the hour is out. Intact and still functioning, if possible. Understood?"

The captain's chin dipped, and he said, "Yes, sir," in a clipped tone that drew a line of gooseflesh down my spine, for I could feel what was beneath it.

Tugging at the lapels of his jacket, the general smoothed his thick hair into submission. "Collect any rebel scum you find," he said. "We're in need of fodder for a royal demonstration, I think."

"Sir."

And then, with a lazy smirk displaying a row of sharp wicked teeth, the general said, "Makes quite an impression, our wildcat, hmm?"

But the captain merely nodded, turning to exit the building with enough speed to leave me reeling in his arms. Dizzy. Clinging to him as everything around me spun and lurched. It was only when the door thumped shut behind us that he murmured, "She's *my* fucking wildcat," under his breath where only I could hear it.

7

———

For a moment, as I hung limp in the captain's arms—nauseous and too weak to do more than breathe—I couldn't make sense of the scene before me.

Sparkling green lightning crackled across the surface of uneven ground, ceaseless and beautiful, even as the scent of burning ozone singed the back of my sinuses. Seeming not to dissipate, it merely moved and jumped and crackled as if the very ground itself was too charged to absorb another drop.

Electrified.

And then I saw it.

Upturned before a massive crater in the earth, an electric blue dome shimmered in the gloomy half-light between dusk and dawn.

The rebel shield.

A glimmering beacon of the rebellion. Technology that shouldn't be possible, but was a testament to the resilience of a people forced into exile but refused to lay down and die.

Elora and Tritan.

Thriving together—there could be no other explanation. Not with the color of that shield.

A direct contrast to the sickly green lightning that seemed not to fade, spidering across the ground beneath me. The whisper of hope, the promise that at least some of Tritan's priestesses had managed to escape the clutches of the empire and dared to fight. To create a thing that had even General Tilcot sweating and slavering at the mere thought of possessing it.

It could only be pure priestess energy.

Similar in texture to the green arcs of elite discharge still clinging to the peaks in churned mud, broken buildings, and the wreckage that was the frontlines—the shield was a magnificent thing. A thing the captain had tried *not* to destroy, if the location of the crater was any sort of indication.

Intact and still functioning, and soon to be in Caledonian hands.

I swallowed, squirming in the captain's embrace, for there, in the distance, movement.

Floundering with the gait of wounded prey, but movement nevertheless.

An Eloran soldier still hiding where he'd been safe, until the captain had been deployed.

Until he'd used my energy to—

"Put me down," I rasped, untangling one leg from the cradle of elite arms.

The captain obliged me, setting my bare feet into the muck. Where green lightning swirled about my ankles for an instant before it sank into my skin. Reviving me with energy that was at once familiar and alien. Mine and his.

Blended together in one confusing soup of power.

I shivered.

Said nothing as my sense of balance returned in gradual surges the longer my feet remained in that hyper-charged muck.

"Gabe," the captain said, and jerked his chin at the Eloran soldier stumbling clear of the shield. "Tilcot wants him alive."

A choked sound slipped from of my lips, but that was all.

Gabe saluted, and said, "Sir," turning to the field with weapon drawn.

I didn't think.

It was as simple as falling back into old habits.

I faked a stumble, landing hard on my knees in the mud. Where my hands were buried to the elbow in grime and rejuvenating elite energy.

"Up you get," the captain murmured, running a soothing, calloused palm down the length of my naked back before scooping me beneath the armpits. "Come. Let's get you into bed, pet."

With a whimper, I let him lift me. My eyes fixed to Marco's boots when the soldier stepped up to the captain's side. Eyes fixed to the distant shield.

It wasn't until I accepted the captain's hand, allowing him help me stand on trembling legs, that I thanked him by yanking Marco's weapon from its holster.

"Oi!" Marco hollered, but I was already gone.

Sprinting through the mud, I whirled. Weapon raised, the captain's stupid, handsome face caught in my sights. And through clenched, bared teeth, I hissed, "Call him off, *Asher*."

For a moment, dark eyes simply watched. Unblinking.

And then, at the corner of his lips, the slightest whisper of a smile flickered to life. A hint of aching burn tingling at my wrists and throat, as if to remind me that he *could* have me on my back in the mud before an audience of his men, but chose not to do it.

"Go ahead," he said, and unbuttoned his sleeves. First the left, then the right. Fingers working over the dark fabric and golden buttons to reveal the wrist cuff that matched my chains—and on the opposite wrist, a matte black one I'd never bothered to notice before. "Take your shot, Mila. You'll only get one."

Icy terror sparkled through my veins, but though my palms had begun to sweat, my grip did not falter. Instead, my gaze flicked back, over my shoulder to the spot where Gabe was frozen midstride. Eyebrows all but buried in his hairline, lips parted in shock as he watched our confrontation unfold.

Forgetting his mission to collect the wounded Eloran and make the man a sacrifice to some faceless Caledonian with royal blood. As I watched, a pair of rebels wearing white sprinted to the field, collecting their fallen in the confusion of my distraction.

And despite the fear, despite knowing that I'd overplayed my hand and earned what was sure to be a dreadful punishment, I smiled. Treasuring this one, tiny victory. In saving just one more from the clutches of the empire.

The captain's attention didn't so much as waver. Not even for an instant. And instead of bothering with the lost victim, he said, "I'm waiting," in a placid drawl that drew my eye back to find a predator shrouded in dark flames. One who'd been held in check too long by duty to his superiors, starved for the hunt while pretending to be the perfect, obedient soldier.

I didn't have to take the bait, so I shrugged and said, "No."

"No?" he returned, soft and deadly. As if there were no one else but the two of us in the entire world. "Don't tell me my warrior priestess has lost her nerve. Here," he said, and took a measured step. "Let me help you."

I adjusted my grip, matching his advance with a

retreat—and tried to toss Marco's weapon into the mud.

Couldn't.

My fingers had seized about the cold, matte metal. The distant tingle all the warning I needed to know that the captain hadn't finished toying with his meal.

He tisked. "Feet braced. Shoulders strong," he cooed, and made me obey. Keeping the deadly end trained directly on his face. "Now take a deep breath," he said, the flames of his wrath igniting behind my ribs when I sucked a breath between my teeth. Feeding him exactly what he craved so badly.

My fear.

"A-Asher, please," I whispered, still backing away no matter the control he kept over my hands.

"I think it's time for another lesson," he said, prowling ever closer. Hips rolling, filth soaking his pants well beyond his ankles. "Pull the trigger," he barked.

It was a command I could not disobey. My fore-arms bunching with the sheer weight of the energy he forced through my muscle, fingers locked tight enough to bruise where they were held at the trigger.

Nothing happened.

Nothing but the thrum of wicked laughter echoed by the men who'd stopped everything to watch the uneven standoff unfold.

"You're missing a few key pieces of that weapon,

pet," he drawled, smirking as Marco lifted his left wrist to display a cuff that matched the color of the weapon now trembling in my grip. "It won't fire for anyone but the owner."

A hitching breath crackled into my lungs as he closed the distance between us at last, putting us all but chest to chest, except for the muzzle of the weapon still held aloft.

I pulled the trigger again. "Bang," I whispered, making a promise only he might hear.

Head thrown back, he laughed. A bark of true amusement that died between the flash of white teeth, but continued to sparkle in those inky, gleaming eyes. "Fire and fury, Mila."

Cheeks flushed hot, I was helpless but to watch as he plucked the weapon from my fingers and tossed it back to Marco. Issuing a scathing, "Can I trust you to handle it from here, or shall I have my priestess take over for you?" over his shoulder.

Marco rubbed the back of his neck, cheeks pink as mine felt. "I should be able to manage without any more distractions from the lady wildcat, sir."

"Good," the captain said, and set rough, needy hands on my skin. Driving me from the mud thick with dancing elite energy back to solid ground. "You and I need to have a little chat," he said, lips pressed to my ear. The rasp of beard stubble making me cower away from heated breath, the hazy threat of a male pressing too close.

I didn't bother to fight him. Couldn't bring myself to spend the energy it would take to make myself heard. I merely walked where he guided, too depleted to do much else.

It wasn't until he sat me in the front seat of Marco's coach that I could bring myself to speak. "The rebels will fight another day."

He hummed, distracted and careless. "That's war, pet." Shifting the vehicle into gear, we glided away from the headquarters building at a much more reasonable pace with the captain behind the wheel. "But the end to this conflict has already been written."

I swallowed the lump lodged at the back of my throat, my eyes flicking left.

He was watching me. A coy smirk promising wicked things I hadn't the stomach to endure after everything that had come before. But no matter the swarm of chaos bubbling in my stomach, I couldn't look away as he navigated through the quiet streets. Careful and precise, his every movement filled with purpose. Intention. Left hand cocked to the left of the wheel, doing the work of steering while the right lay braced on the armrest between us. Fourth finger picking at his thumbnail as if anxious for what came next.

"So what's my big punishment?" I asked, quiet in the gloomy silence. "Or are you waiting until we're alone?" Lip curled, I sneered, arms crossed beneath my breasts to cover the shiver of nerves I couldn't quite repress. "Afraid to let anyone see what you actually are?"

He glanced at me, brow cocked. "You'd rather I fuck you before an audience? Because that can certainly be arranged." He laughed, low and bitter. Knuckles going white around the wheel. "I've got nothing but time, after all. Now that I'm off duty. Who knows? Maybe I can distract Tilcot's interest in you by turning you into my personal whore. We can perform nightly shows for the men under the guise of boosting morale. Maybe then he'll only want a turn, instead of plotting how he might take you for himself in the name of the empire. I'm sure he's penning a letter to the Capitol even now, citing your blatant disobedience as just cause."

He threw the vehicle into park. Exiting without a word, he disappeared from sight only to pop up at my door, wrenching it open hard enough to make the hinges squeal a mechanical protest.

"What's the difference?" I asked, and took his hand without complaint. Jaw tight, shoulders bunched with tension as he herded me up the steps of his stolen residence. "You both mean to use me to kill, and so I hate you both equally."

The captain snorted and plunged us into darkness with the *snick* of the front door clicking shut. "And what exactly can you do to stop it, priestess?" he hummed, looming over my shoulder, at my back, where his words could be felt against my jaw.

I flinched, but to this, I had nothing to say. Not yet.

Marching me past the hall-stand, he slipped his hands around my ribs and lifted me without another word.

I gasped, ready to fight until I heard the distinct crunch of broken glass and plaster beneath his boots. My bare feet touching down on the hardwood clear of slicing danger—feet that paced beyond the small kitchen, up the stairs, down the hall, and into his personal quarters.

"Stay," he snapped when I stood outside of his private bathroom. Disappearing to the sound of running water splashing in a basin.

Unable to so much as fidget, I turned my focus instead to the uncomfortable hum living in my wrists and throat. Watching the subtle glow illuminating my veins with a new perspective. One that whispered of dangers I couldn't see lurking inside.

An empath.

Dangerous.

Too volatile be allowed free reign amongst the priestesses or the elites.

Eyes burning with some unknown, distant pain, I blinked.

Clenching my fists until my nails pressed deep into the meat of my palms, I tired to touch that unspoken hurt lashing at my heart. To know what it was.

"Here," the captain said, moving on feet silent enough to startle. "Sit."

I blinked up at him in the gloom. "Where—"

One damp hand landed on my collarbone, pushing me back without bothering to exert his influence. Pushing until my thighs hit the mattress and I sat without meaning to.

For a moment, he loomed above me. Inky eyes gleaming with the spark of ravenous flames. Tense and watchful all at once.

And then he knelt.

Bumping my knees apart, he settled between my thighs and let his fingers trail down. Over the swell of my left breast, smirking when my breath caught, though he moved on too quickly to do more than make my cheeks flush. His touch drifting over the ridges of my ribs, tracing the entire length of my thigh until he reached my knee. Until his fingers found bare skin.

But still, he didn't stop until he'd caught my ankle in the heat of his palm.

Something warm and wet slapped over my foot.

A wash cloth.

Wiping away the mud caked on my skin, he worked the rough fabric between my toes, paying careful attention to the spots that made me flinch and squirm.

Frozen, I could only watch. Unblinking. Shocked still and compliant as he worked.

When he'd finished with the left, his fingers shot up. Gripping my calf, he threw my ankle over his shoulder and left me spread. My skirts stretched taut, hands thrown back to brace, I couldn't speak. Not with my heart clawing at the back of my throat, hammering away at my senses in an erratic flail that robbed me of all sense.

Without a word, his attention moved to the other side. Thumbs tracing maddening little circles in the arch of my foot, he wiped away the worst of the mud. Eyes fixed to his chosen task, he left me to shiver in the dark.

To watch as he worked and try to gather my wits.

He tossed the soiled cloth over his shoulder, letting it land with a careless splat.

And then, for the first time, he glanced up. Inky eyes catching on what lay in shadows, he paused at the gap between my knees.

Nostrils flared.

Lips parted on a silent inhale.

Almost unable to draw breath, belly rigid with the tension to hold myself upright with the bulk of my weight braced on my palms, I shivered. Flinching when both of his hands slid over my hips. Rising up, bunching my skirts as he dipped in close. His nose skimming up, between my breasts, over the hollow at the base of my throat, and settled behind my ear.

Rough hands rolled over my waist, fingers spanning the narrow dip between hip and rib, he squeezed where I was soft before the calloused rasp traced the entire length of my spine. He drew me close. Fingertips skating up with a purpose until his fingers found the tie at the back of my neck.

He pulled.

Black silk spilled over my chest, baring me to eyes gone bottomless with greed.

I yelped.

Flopping back, my left arm shot out to cup one breast. My forearm smushing the other, secreting it away from inspection. And with my free hand, I pressed against the expanse of hard, male chest that surged over me. "Asher—"

"Just can't help yourself, can you?" he drawled, and caught my wrist. Claiming the space I'd tried to force him to abandon, he pinned my right hand high above my head and set his gaze on the only scrap of protection I had left. "Can't help but fight your nature, no matter that you've already well and truly lost," he murmured, eyes tracing the fatty swell I hid beneath my palm. Under my forearm. "But most of all," he said, and drew my fingers back. One at a time, plucking them free of that final, guarded treasure until I lay bare before him. "You can't help the way you ache for more, can you?"

I swallowed, *hard*. Back arching when he stretched my left hand high above my head.

Securing my wrists to the mattress in one palm, he pinned me with his weight. Settling between my thighs so he might admire the pale skin gleaming in the darkness.

Even through the fabric of his uniform, I felt him lurch against me. Felt a length of blunt, steely flesh kick and fight for the freedom to ravage.

But I didn't beg.

Didn't cry or whimper.

I didn't have to, for it was that moment my stomach yowled in protest. Days of neglect whining in shameless submission, pleading mercy for all the meals I'd missed in the chaos following my capture.

He laughed. Free hand falling to the hollow between my ribs, where my stomach bubbled, he grinned at me in the dark. "Hungry for something more than cock, pet?"

"You're a pig," I whispered, but my stomach snarled again, against his palm.

Forehead dipping, he sucked in a breath that trembled, paused long enough to gather himself, then untangled us. He left me there, all but naked, spread on tidy sheets. "Such a pretty picture," he said, stuffing one hand down the front of his slacks, adjusting the length that promised to leave me in ruins. "Stay put," he cooed, and let his influence surge to life one more. Keeping me still, even as he turned and disappeared from sight.

It wasn't until he was gone that I took my turn to

draw a ragged breath. Heart slowing in his absence, the exhaustion flooded in.

And, unable to scrub at the burning itch that made my eyes water, I simply squeezed them shut. Blocking everything out.

The hunger...

The slippery ache...

The storm of elite havoc rampaging through my blood.

All of it lost to the blackness behind my eyelids.

I was asleep before he returned.

My last thought not to wonder at what I might be, but a dreadful realization.

With my help, the Elorans had claimed their injured man from the field, but in doing so they'd left the shield in Caledonian hands...

8

Wrapped in a cocoon of warmth, I slept. Entranced by swirling, murky blackness that yawned and hummed a drowsy song. A song of sedation and warmth and hypnotic beauty. And behind my ribs, the heat of dark flames licking and pulling. *Burning* in the pit of my stomach, where I ached to be indulged, my hunger relieved.

It only grew worse. Growling long and low in the silence stuffing my ears, begging for food. For things I couldn't begin to name.

I rolled to ignore the hunger pains. Writhing in silken sheets, I burrowed deeper, thighs whispering over luxury I hadn't known in... years. Skin bare and cool despite the heat pulsing through my veins.

Groaning, I curled around myself. Flexed my back and snuggled beneath the soothing weight.

Blankets saturated in an intoxicating scent, one I drew deep into my lungs, face pressed into a feathered pillow.

Hands dipping between my thighs, I clasped my palms and squeezed my knees together. Warming my fingers. Seeking comfort in a place where such a thing was rare to the point of absurdity.

Instead, I found the ache of slick flesh.

The urge to press against everything that was hard and cruel. *Possessive.* Taking things I couldn't give.

I gasped.

Cold sweat prickling my hairline, my eyes snapped open to stare at nothing. Sightless, until I blinked and sucked a breath between sagging jaws.

I was panting.

Hungry and confused.

Naked.

Starved for a thing I had only been made to taste.

Teeth bared, I kicked free of tangled, cloying sheets and sprang from the bed. A blur of pale, naked skin. Sides heaving with exertion, as if I'd been running through summer's thick, muggy heat.

Eyes darting about the darkened room, I stood with fists clenched at my sides. Trembling, every muscle taut with tension, trying to take in my surroundings, to find a weapon before I was discovered awake and alone in the captain's private quarters.

But what I found wasn't the sinister den of torment I'd thought it to be. Illuminated by early morning sunlight, what had previously been concealed in shadow was nothing more than a richly appointed bedroom. A man's sparse sense of decoration, void of color that wasn't the traditional Caledonian black and gold. Furnished without a whisper of clutter.

A space that was far less threatening *without* the captain in it.

Heading for the en suit bathroom, I relieved myself in private. Grateful for the luxury of amenities after so long living in the wood, yet not daring to flush for fear of drawing attention to myself.

At least, not until I'd dressed. Until I was armed with something more than pointless begging that fell on merciless ears.

Rummaging through the captain's personal effects, I found military uniforms, clothing that reeked of luxury, but not so much as a stitch even remotely close to my size. Not even the dreadful slave silks he'd dressed me in the last time I'd woken in this room with no idea how I'd come to be here.

"Try the closet," said a snide voice.

I whirled with fists clenched, feet braced shoulder width apart before I thought to hide my nudity.

Beau.

Sneering around a truly spectacular bruise that matched the imprint of my knuckles, the elderly slave let milky eyes wander over my breasts—cataloguing everything else below them—making sure I could see just how unimpressive I really was. "You'll be wanting another bath, I'm sure. The master doesn't tolerate the stench of sour pussy on his whores."

I smiled, showing teeth before I turned and pulled a sheet off the bed, ignoring the vulgar slur. "What's it like?" I asked instead, and took my time in dressing. Eyes fixed to her every subtle movement, searching for the weakness I could sense lurking just beyond sight.

One grey brow rose as she stooped to retrieve a rumpled garment. "I beg your pardon?"

"You helped to give him a priestess. A prized resource growing more fleeting with every passing hour." I shrugged, head cocked as I watched her pick up after her master, one hand twisted in the fabric bunched over my chest. "What's it like to know you'll never achieve anything more significant than that? Do you just... wait for death, or is there some other purpose you might fulfill? I can't imagine there's much in the way of demand for a retired whore that's... *well*." My eyes flicked down her body, returning her gracious sentiment. "But we *are* deep inside the Empire of Caledonia, so what could I really know about it?"

She spluttered, face going waxy. "You insolent little girl! I've dedicated a lifetime in service to the Rawlings bloodline, and—"

"And all I have to do is breathe," I said, "and I'm more important than you'll ever be." I took a step toward her, sheets trailing along in my wake as I paced closer. Filling my lungs with a delicious aroma I was becoming intimately familiar with.

Righteous fury—the scent so thick in the air I could taste it. Could feel the heat of such indignant angst that I was moved to warm myself in the crackle of dark flames. To feed from the perfume wafting from deep inside her aging body until it became something new.

Fear.

Her face flushed an ugly shade that clashed with her bruised eye socket.

But I spoke before she could strain herself too much, a feral, toothy smile spreading across my lips. "No one's here to save you this time, Beau. But... would anyone really notice if something... *sinister* were to happen here today? Would anyone care, or would you be replaced before anyone thought to question your absence?"

"Thank you, Beau," the captain said, and shattered the spell. Arms crossed, shoulder braced against the doorframe, he watched me through a narrow glare. "You may take the rest of the day for yourself, but please send Alicia, will you? Mila needs an escort."

She nodded, and without a word, fled. Defeated. The shine of wetness visible on her blotchy cheeks.

The captain pushed off the doorframe. "That was some truly inspired cruelty, pet. Care to pick a fight with a more worthy opponent?"

I retreated with a curled lip. Knees soft, coiled for the coming battle I fully intended to provoke, I clutched the fabric closer to my breasts. "Don't you have a war to wage on innocent citizens? Oh, that's right," I said, refusing to give up my back. "You're Captain Asher Rawlings. The impotent soldier who can't fight."

The crackle of ravenous energy blazed in my core. Demanding to be fed. To feast until there was nothing left.

"Funny girl," he drawled, advancing on silent feet. "But now that I'm off duty, I've all the time in the world to dedicate to training my unruly priestess." He took another rolling step, insatiable greed crackling in the air between us. "My little empath."

Muscles tense, I watched him without blinking.

"I've got you all to myself," he drawled, obsidian eyes gleaming in the half-light. Taunting me. "And there's no one," he murmured with a smirk, "who's coming to save you, Mila. Not this time."

With a sneer, I stepped to the side—and the sheet got tangled between my feet.

The captain didn't hesitate.

He lunged, catching my shoulders. Strong, blunt fingertips bit deep into the muscle, and dark eyes flicked down. To the hand locked tight around the makeshift knot concealing my nudity—a weakness he meant to exploit.

He grinned. Leering as if he hadn't already seen everything I had to offer.

I thrashed. "Get off—"

The words died on my tongue, a gasp caught high at the back of my throat.

Power.

It licked through me in a swirl, tasting. *Taking.* Infecting me with the pulsing, ravenous burn of elite poison that seeped through my blood and marrow, touching everything I was. Tainting and twisting it.

He sucked a breath through parted lips. Head falling back, so he might watch me from beneath a hooded glare and lowered lashes.

"Don't touch me," I snarled, trying to writhe free from his grip.

The rumble of deep, mocking laughter spilled over his lips. "But Mila," he drawled, and sent his energy deeper, feeding the poisonous hunger he'd left behind my ribs, "you *want* me to touch you."

It was my turn to laugh. "I can assure you, I'd prefer death," I spat, flashing pointed teeth. Standing strong before the monster who ruled me without flinching.

Caught in his snare, I was helpless when his fingers abandoned my shoulders. When they traveled up, to cup both sides of my skull, dwarfing me in big palms that cradled when they might have crushed.

"You think I can't feel that?" he whispered, thumbs tipping my head back to expose my throat. "How badly you need it." He stepped forward, driving me back. "The way you ache to be filled. Stuffed and stretched." A smirk danced in inky eyes when he stooped to press his lips to my ear. "Because I can. And I know exactly how much you hate yourself for wanting it."

Outrage made me snarl, "It's *you*! I can't get your filthy, elite poison out of my head!" But when he chuckled, I lunged. Incensed. Aiming to sink my teeth into the vulnerable, exposed flesh of his throat.

The rasp of his beard grated against my skin. "There's my wildcat," he hummed, blocking me with humiliating ease before he sent nimble fingers to pluck at the sheets. Jerking them from my grip, he sent the flutter of dark silk tumbling to the floor, making me scramble to hide. Vulnerable, exposed to his every lewd whim. And without giving me a chance to recover or stoop, he spun me. Sent me staggering forward, to land with palms braced on the edge of his mattress.

He was on me before I could take another breath. "I can't stop thinking about it," he rasped, pinning me in the way he liked. With his weight at my back and the furious beat of aroused male kicking at the ache between my legs. "Can't stop imagining what it'll be like to watch you choke on my cock."

"Try it," I snarled, and bucked against his chest. "I'll bite it off at the root."

Blunt teeth set against the meat of my shoulder, his breath a tiny, heated explosion of amusement. "I wonder," he said, ignoring me without bothering to exert his influence, "if you'll beg for it when I let you breathe." One hand slipped over my hip, grating over the sensitive skin beneath my bellybutton before he found my mound. Hairless and swollen. He cupped me in the heat of his palm, his fingers pressing a gentle threat against my folds, lingering without seeking more. "I wonder if you'll drip for me when I come down your throat and make you drink every last drop."

I whined, head sagging, my shoulder blades growing sharp as I strained to bare his weight and mine. Trembling beneath the onslaught of alien arousal pumping through my veins. "Never," I said, breathless, the sound fragile and pathetic even to my own ears.

"Oh, I don't know about *never*," he cooed, and spread those fingers. Letting slick heat spill over invasive digits, he stole a breath from the hair at my nape. "It's so easy for me to infect you, after all," he said, derisive and cruel, plunging two hooked fingers inside. "A pussy this wet couldn't *possibly* be because you want to get fucked raw by an enemy, right? It's all this elite energy I'm wielding."

Legs trembling, I tried to drag a breath through

the clog in my throat, but managed only a tiny sip. My back twisting beneath his weight. Writhing against the ache of being stretched by thick fingers.

"This is all *my* fault," he continued, and pulled back just to make me listen. So I might hear the liquid squelch as his fingers worked, before plunging back inside. Deeper, this time. Curled against a spot that drew the swollen lips of my sex apart on a silent gasp as sweat beaded across my forehead. "This pretty little cunt sings for *me*, not you. Isn't that right?"

I shook my head, a soundless denial whispering across my lips.

It was enough to make him laugh. Shoving me face-down into the sheets, his free hand moved to work at his belt, to unleash that length of angry flesh. "Shit," he rasped after a pause, and I felt his fist pump against my thigh. Felt the blunt kiss of something hot and sticky where it bumped my skin, fist moving in time with his fingers. Making a mess of the slick treachery pouring from my slit.

Calves burning, I squirmed and tried to crawl for freedom. Every ounce of my bravado long gone, to be replaced by stark, raw instinct. "Please."

"Begging already?" he said, and pulled his fingers free. "I must admit, I'm a touch disappointed. Thought my warrior priestess would be harder to break." Abandoning his thick length, he tangled his fingers in my hair and held me still. Cheek pressed into the sheets, he showed me the evidence of what he'd done between my thighs, holding glistening fingers up to the dim light. "But this couldn't possibly be *you,* could it?"

Tears spilled over my lashes, then. The brine swallowed up by dark fabric, my cheeks hot, I panted for breath.

"Taste it then," he whispered, and painted my tongue. "Taste what I did to you and tell me how much you don't want this. I'll wait."

Something in my chest shattered at the tangy sweetness, and without pausing to think, I twisted. Lunged for the meat of his wrist, and sank my teeth into the muscle with a desperate sob.

He cursed, and with crushing force, the full bulk of a furious male fell across my back. Pressing every last sip of air from my lungs. "Let go," he whispered, voice tight with the unmistakable edge of pain.

I shook my head. Rallying free of the seductive lure he'd spun through my brain.

"No?" he asked, and I shook my head again, smiling against his flesh when my teeth sank ever deeper. When the salty tang of blood flooded my mouth and replaced the deepest shame I might imagine with the rush of vengeance. "Fine," he whispered, and snaked one hand between us, despite the grip I had on his flesh. Lining himself up—pumping once, *twice,* saturating himself in cream—he pressed rigid arousal into my melting flesh. Poised to take every last piece of me, he called my bluff, and said, "Then play time is over."

I squealed, releasing him as I tried to claw my way to freedom. "A-Asher," I cried, trying to bend my knees, to escape the heavy pall fogging my senses before it was too late.

He bucked against me with a fractured groan, the whisper of dark flames surging to life at the sound of his name on my lips. "I'm going to make you gape for me," he whispered, hips pressing forward. *Deeper.* "You'll feel it," he rasped, one hand sweeping down, to lift my right thigh and leave my bent knee on the mattress. Leaving me wide open as he looked on. "In every step you take for the next week, you'll feel me drip from this cunt and know who owns you."

Eyes squeezed shut, I shivered. Clawing at the sheets. "I may be bound to you," I rasped, breath hitching when he peeled slick lips apart, his thumb pressing the head of his shaft down, so it might pierce through all that was throbbing and untouched. "But I'll n-never be yours."

His hand settled on my hip, grip tight enough to bruise all the way through the fat and deep into my muscle.

And then he pressed forward to make his claim, to show me just how wrong I was without bothering to speak a single word. Stretching. Branding me from the inside as he stuffed every slow inch of himself inside me.

"This means n-nothing," I gasped, hiccuping through the worst of it. The ache that begged to be submitted. Tamed. "O-only that I had the bad l-luck to be found by you first." Burying my face into the blanket, I shuddered as he broke through the last of my restraint, sliding all the way to my roof. Where he struck something too deep and stole my breath.

"Fuck*sakes*," he snarled, not unmoved. Shivering at my back, where I couldn't see. Could only feel the crackle of elite energy when it burned with desperate need. "So fucking tight. So—*hnggh*—so wet."

I sucked a shaking breath between my lips and struck a blow meant to wound. "I wish it was the general," I whispered, my words scarcely more than a breath. My heart in tatters. "I wish General Tilcot had found me first. At least *he'd* be my equal."

For a moment, the captain was still. Buried to the hilt, stretching me in ways I'd never thought possible, he filled me to the brim but still had more to give.

And then he surged forward.

Catching my right wrist in an unforgiving grip, he wrenched my arm behind my back. Twisting my forearm until he'd forced my fingers to sit between my shoulder blades, he bucked into me only to withdraw. To shift, slotting his right knee under mine— forcing me to brace on one leg as he pulled back and kept me off balance as he mounted me. He bucked back inside in a single, brutal thrust that dragged a ragged little scream from my lips.

"You want to be treated like a whore?" he snarled, fucking into me with all the fury coursing through his blood. The wounded pride. "Is that it? You want to be fucked like a sleeve? Used by whoever earns a turn?"

Eyes bulging, I couldn't speak. Couldn't breathe or fight. I could only lay there, pinned, speared, and helpless, as I took what I had provoked. My blood saturated with *him*.

My body.

Every erratic beat of my heart wound me tighter, pulling me deeper into the flames until I was burning with it. Aching and hurting for a thing I couldn't name.

"Do you want to be like Sasha?" he spat, and hooked his forearm beneath my chin. Every heaving, blistering inch of muscle surging against my back, my trapped wrist locked in place by the weight of his chest. "Beaten down. *Broken*," he growled, beard rasping against my cheek. "A shell of the woman she was. A walking ghost who's seen what horror really is."

"A-Asher," I gasped, small and weak, and felt him grow impossibly hard. Felt him swell inside me, at the base, where he stretched my opening. "Please—" I clutched at his forearm, needing mercy. Needing relief or torment.

"Fine," he spat, and picked up a punishing rhythm. Giving exactly what I couldn't ask for, he sat back. Perched between my thighs, where both hands found purchase on my hips, and he forced me to bend. Forced my pelvis to tip forward, to open for him as he fucked me breathless. "Then beg for my come, slave," he snarled, riding me toward a crest. Gliding seamlessly in and out, he worked himself into a furious lather. "Tell me exactly what you need."

I couldn't.

Couldn't name it, had no idea how to speak or where to begin.

I could only sob a wordless plea and pray for relief.

With a snarl, he drove into me with one final, punishing thrust. "Take it," he spat, and pulsed as deep inside as he could get. Sending jet after jet of searing hot seed to splash against the entrance to my womb, twitching as he pumped me full.

"You're going to come on this dick," he growled, and slipped one hand over my hip and found the bead of my achingly swollen clit. "I want you to milk my balls dry," he said, and rolled that bundle of nerves between two fingers. Sending a tendril of smoldering, dark energy straight into my tender, traumatized flesh.

Squealing, I tried to buck him off. Panicked by the flood threatening to drown me. "I-I can't—"

"You *will*," he hissed, sluicing through my folds. Bumping the place deep inside that overwhelmed my every sense. "I can feel it coming," he whispered, taunting me. "You're shaking. So fucking tight it makes me want to come all over again." Picking up speed, he worked my clit. Strumming it at the perfect pace. "I want to feel you come for me, pet. Do it," he snarled, and wrapped strong fingers around the base of my throat.

My every muscle seized as the wave crashed. As he sent a tsunami of elite energy into my over-wrought system and forced a brutal orgasm to wrench through my body.

"Oh, *fuck*," he rasped, and I felt him pulse inside me all over again. Caught in the storm of his own making, he rode me though it with ragged breaths and clenching hands. Utterly overwhelmed by the convulsions he'd demanded milk him dry.

Shuddering to a stop, he collapsed across my back.

Heart thudding in time with mine.

Sweat pooling between his chest and my back.

Our fluids mixed.

And then, setting his teeth to my shoulder, he marked me. Pinching the muscle where any might see it and know what it meant.

That I'd been bred from the back.

Fucked raw by my enemy.

"Your cunt is mine," he said, and kneaded my breast, catching one beaded nipple between fore-finger and thumb. Twisting until I moaned, squirming and sliding around his girth. "Mine to mark." Hips still pumping, he lingered. Taking lewd pleasure in the mess of bitter cream seeping around his base. "Mine to fill. To punish and spoil. *All mine.*"

A hitching breath stuttered into my lungs, but that was all.

"I should make you lick it clean," he murmured, beard rasping against my cheek. My ear. A gentle caress before his voice grew hard and he withdrew in a rush that left me reeling, scrambling for an anchor. "But you're due at the general's manse. Lucky you."

My supporting leg turned to water, and I crumpled. Boneless. Nearly sinking to the floor before my hips took the bulk of my weight and I hung from the edge of the mattress. Reddened bottom on full, indecent display. Dripping, *throbbing.* Unable to really comprehend what he'd said, to decipher the bitter spite lashing against my back.

"Mmm," he groaned, and slipped two fingers back inside. Playing in the mess, he spread his fingers and pried my passage open.

Made me gape.

A flood of wetness seeped out.

"Now *that's* a pretty picture," he said, smearing himself all over my mound. His thumb pressing against the tight ring of muscle that guarded my ass. Prodding without penetrating.

I hadn't even the strength to muster a protest.

"Get up," he said, and, tone shifting to an unmistakable order, he abandoned me with a hard slap on the ass. Fingers leaving me to gush and drip in his absence. "You're to spend the day training with Sasha."

I blinked.

Exhaled.

Still twitching around the phantom stretch and wriggle moving behind my pelvic bone.

Something wet splattered against the carpet, and I blushed. Heat searing my cheeks enough to motivate me to move.

Crawling, I lifted myself. Turned, and sat on the edge of the mattress, no doubt leaving a mess on the sheets beneath my nudity. A mess Beau would be around to straighten before night fell. Dizzy as I heard him rummaging through his closet. Unseen, only to return fully dressed, if a little rumpled. Over his left forearm, a length of now familiar black silks, edged in gold.

I swallowed, unable to meet his eye. Both hands gripping the mattress at my hips, I focused instead on remaining upright. On giving him nothing more to hold over me.

Unfolding the silks with a snap of his wrist, he draped the complicated wrap around my shoulders and twisted. A different iteration on what I'd been wearing the day before, he gave me both modesty and left me feeling utterly exposed.

He pulled me to my feet, grinning when I wobbled. When he had to keep me stable until I had both knees locked and I could stand without him. "Come," he said, and those dark eyes grew tight with tension once more.

I took one step, thighs gliding together with the slippery gush oozing from my bruised and swollen pussy.

A humorless huff of air crossed my lips, and I turned in a swirl of dark silk. Chin held high, I headed straight for the en suit bathroom.

"And where," he asked, pacing at my side, "do you think you're going, hmm?"

"To scourge your filth off me."

Another quick, predatory grin flicked across his lips, and he said, simply, "No," and steered me toward the exit.

Feet braced, I tried to stop. "Asher—"

"You're going to the general's manse," he said, and his fingers found their grip on the back of my neck. His lips ghosting against my ear. "And you're going to do it with *my* come dripping from that tight cunt," he whispered. "All day long. If you think you can throw yourself at the general in some misguided attempt to escape, you can do it reeking of sour, used pussy."

9

Quiet voices wafted up from the lower floor, and with one hand on my nape, the captain paused on the upper landing. Inspecting the bloody imprint of my teeth sunk deep into the flesh of his wrist. Above the ring of matte black that apparently controlled his weapon.

He flexed, scowling at the damage.

And with a tiny crease between his brows, his attention shifted... inside.

I felt it turn.

The crackle of searing elite energy grew soft, the edges smoothed. Tempered by something cool and soothing. A change of the tides that lapped at the damage I'd wrought and made it whole. Knitting broken flesh, mending a lacerated tendon.

"That's not possible," I breathed, head spinning

with the implications of an elite wielding the gifts of a priestess. Healing himself with a talent he had no rights to possess.

The captain grinned, clenching his fist just to watch the smooth glide of his now-undamaged wrist work the way it should. "Sweet, innocent Mila," he drawled, and rolled his sleeve into place. Fixing the buttons with a twist of nimble fingers that had my cheeks heating in sordid memory. "So ignorant. So blind."

Head still spinning—thighs wet and legs wobbly —I couldn't muster the will to argue.

Because there was no denying what I'd just seen him do.

I simply went where he guided, one hand firm on my nape. Careful on the stairs, my head in a fog of shocked numbness.

"Good morning, captain," Alicia murmured, offering a demure dip of her chin. Eyes downcast.

A shiver ignited in my blood at the sight.

Something angry and tense that longed to lash out and inflict damage.

"Alicia," the captain returned with a nod, his dark eyes flicking over her shoulder to land on the two soldiers at her back. Marco with his long legs crossed at the ankle, lounging in the kitchen picking at a platter of fruits and vegetables, and Gabe, standing rigid as the captain entered.

The captain jerked his chin, and without a word

the soldiers followed. Moving to the opposite side of the kitchen to have a quiet conversation.

"Good morning, priestess," Alicia said.

Jaw tight, I scowled at the floor. Ignoring the traitor standing before me. My fists clenched, knuckles white.

She cleared her throat. "You should have something to eat before we go. Beau said—"

I scoffed, marching toward the door to wait where I wouldn't be plagued by the sight of her face. The sound of her voice laced with the tender lies of someone who'd learned to mimic true concern or affection.

"Mila"—she kept pace with me, daring to touch my shoulder—"wait. Please."

"Get your hand off me," I spat, forcing the words through the points of my modified canines. Trembling, my cheeks hot. Heart pounding away at the backside of my ribs.

She jerked her hand back, cheeks blanched a satisfying shade of waxy white. "Eat something," she said, and showed me the apple clenched in her free hand.

For a moment, I merely continued to glare. Letting her see the truth, that her every breath was an insult I wished to extinguish, but couldn't because she'd sold me to my enemy for nothing more than a pat on the head. A scratch behind the ears.

And then I turned. Giving up my back to an

insignificant threat. An advantage I knew she'd never take, lest she disobey her precious master. The rumble of my stomach an easy thing to ignore for spite.

Her breath caught, and with no small amount of forged concern, she said, "Was he rough?"

My spine stiffened.

Delicate fingers found a sore spot on my shoulder, prodding a distinct ring of bruises I'd forgotten to hide.

I jerked as if scalded, my back thumping to hit the door as I spun. One hand pressed over the imprint of the captain's teeth. His mark on my skin.

Alicia's keen gaze flicked over my face. Taking note of high, flushed cheeks. Tangled hair. Swollen, puffy eyes rimmed in red. Every detail that screamed the truth of what had happened to one who knew just what to look for.

A whore.

Like recognizing like.

Breath coming in hard, short gasps, I collapsed in on myself. Shoulders curling, arms wrapped around the vulnerable spots—my chest and belly, anywhere that threatened to burst wide open in an explosion of panic and gore—trying to protect from further attack.

Alicia's eyes went wide. "It was your first time."

It wasn't a question.

And I had nothing to say. No voice to combat the

disgusting edge of pity that crinkled her elegant edges. No pressing urge to deny her realization.

There was only the screaming silence echoing between my ears.

"Ready?" Marco asked, making us both jump.

One hand pressed to her heart, Alicia said, "Shit, Marco!" in a breathless whisper. "Give a girl some warning before you creep up on her."

"I like that you don't know when I'm coming, beautiful," Marco said, and rubbed her shoulders.

She brushed him off with a glittering, good-natured smile. The mimic's mask sliding back into place. "That's what all the girls say about you."

A choked, wounded sound came from Marco's throat, and he said, "How 'bout you, wildcat?" with a friendly bump of his hip. "Anything cruel to say to poor old Marco this morning?"

I dipped under his arm and padded into the street on bare feet without a word. Ignoring the sting of cold cobblestones against my skin, I dragged a breath through my lips. Forcing my lungs to expand no matter how inflexible they'd become.

"See, Alicia?" Marco hummed, closing the door with a deft click. "The wildcat knows how to show a little respect."

"Nah, sorry, mate," Gabe said. "She's just learned to filter out your voice, that's all." Without tainting his stoic exterior, Gabe glanced down the busy street and unclipped his weapon as he scanned the area.

Alicia cleared her throat. "You know, I bet that's it. But"—she licked her lips—"before we head over to the manse, we need to make a detour to the bathhouse first. Mila could use a nice soak—"

"Sorry, beautiful," Marco said, and slung his arm about her shoulders. "Can't. The lady wildcat is due for training. Not stops. We're to go straight there, and come straight back. Captain's orders."

Swallowing the humiliated ache clawing at the back of my throat, I let my eyes fall before Alicia might see the truth. That the captain *wanted* me soiled and claimed. Reeking of his seed as a means of warding off any other interested males.

I tuned them all out. Reeling and untethered, my feet carrying me forward long after my mind had withdrawn. The walls of my reality crumbling all around me to reveal a place where an elite could heal himself. Where a man I hated could do exactly what he pleased with my body, and I was left to suffer the sticky, swollen consequences.

I caught a choked sob between my molars, grinding it into submission until I could taste bitter, crushed enamel.

And so it was that I was caught unaware, finding myself standing in the great, sweeping front hall of the general's manse with no recollection as to how I'd come to be there.

The Head Priestess stood with hands folded

before her, waiting. A serene smile gracing bruised lips.

My eyes flicked over her face and I saw that damage in a new light, the captain's cruel words mocking as he drove me into the mattress.

Fucked like a sleeve. Used. Beaten down by horror. A ghost still clinging to a broken shell...

Inclining her head, she turned and gestured for us to follow as she navigated the grand halls, moving on the balls of her feet as if afraid to make a single sound. She didn't stop to admire any of the stolen treasures. Didn't seem to see the paintings or the sculptures.

She walked.

We followed.

Until a thick oak door drew her to a stop.

"Ladies," Gabe said and pushed it open with a tight bow.

She motioned for me to proceed her into the tiny dark room, and said, "Thank you for the escort, gentlemen. Alicia."

Marco caught the door before she could close it in his face. "We've been given direct orders not to leave Mila's side." Holstering his weapon, he moved to enter the tight room.

One elegant, silver-blonde brow raised, the Head Priestess glanced around. "And where, might I ask, do you intend to sit as you guard her safety from inside a windowless room, in the heart of General Tilcot's estate?"

"I, uhh—" Marco blushed, pushing a fist through the mussy hair at the back of his head.

"You know that's not what he meant, Sasha," Gabe said, calm yet firm, maintaining eye contact as he hovered on the threshold.

A flicker of something made of steel gleamed in icy blue eyes. "The training of a young priestess—let alone an empath—is a sacred thing requiring a peaceful environment free of distractions. I'm sorry, but it's just not possible for any of you to be here for this."

Marco shifted with an uneasy look. "We've got our orders, Sasha."

"And I've got mine from General Harper Tilcot, whom I believe outranks a mere captain. But you're more than welcome to interrupt his day to find out. Or go stand guard outside the door," she said, "where you can easily do both. I can assure you, Mila will be perfectly safe behind this unlocked door."

Casting a final, uneasy glance at each other, the soldiers shuffled back. And the last thing I saw before the Head Priestess closed a flimsy barrier between us and them, was the brilliant green of Alicia's eyes. Intense, as if trying to convey some hidden message I had no intention of heeding.

For a moment, there was the blessed ring of

silence. Uncomfortable, but edged with a soft hum I thought to be peace.

"Please," she said, and spread her hands toward a plush, if worn white chair. "Take a seat."

"How do I get these fucking manacles off?" I snarled, shivering despite the lack of airflow in the tiny, warm space.

With a sigh, she settled into the only other piece of furniture in the room—a hard-backed wooden chair. "You can't. Believe me," she whispered, and folded her hands, "I've tried."

A tremor started deep inside my chest. "Can *they* take them off, then?"

She didn't bother to reply. Simply watched me pace from behind her desk.

And then, "You look... thin, Mila. Ragged."

I curtsied, and the action was more brittle than the snappy, "Thank you," that spattered over my lips. Shoulders bunched, I did another lap, the ache of tension making my jaw throb, for with every step, I could feel the pulse of tacky brine still oozing from where I'd been filled. Violated and ruined. My every jagged thought tracking back to *him* as I fingered the crescent bruises beginning to purple on my shoulder. "If I can't be free of the chains, then tell me how to kill him."

The Head Priestess folded her hands. Lips thin and white before she said, "You can't."

"Then give me another solution, Head Priestess,

because I can't live with being his slave, and I won't be a weapon for the empire. I *won't*." A tremor raced through my blood. Hot and ravenous, it twisted in my chest before I stilled, focused on her face with an unblinking stare. Lip curled. "Frankly, I don't know how you've done it for so long."

"Sasha," she murmured, matching all that toxic fury with a placid stare that was serene. Utterly absent so much as a whisper of fear, she refused to rise to the challenge.

I blinked. "What?"

"Call me Sasha." Her lips twitched around a fragile smirk. "I haven't been the Head Priestess in five years. Sasha will suffice."

Rolling my neck, I flexed my shoulder blades. "Fine, Sasha, how do I kill him?"

"You're an empath," she replied. "Bound to an elite."

I resumed my pacing, hardly able to wait for her to finish evading the question.

"You're tied to everything around you," she went on, elaborating. Measuring her words at an agonizing pace. "To the captain now, too. *Deeply.*"

"Then it'll be that much more satisfying to watch the life fade from his eyes," I snarled, salivating at the thought of watching those inky, bottomless depths go flat and blank. Everything he was, extinguished.

She ignored me. "Every living thing has energy. A life force. Something only a priestess can touch," she murmured, and stood. Taking a slow step, she mirrored my posture with one that was soothing. Muscles at ease. A leisurely stroll that opposed my erratic pacing. "It is our divine gift to touch the life around us and know what it is beneath. To redirect sickness and rot and give it new purpose."

"I'm no healer," I snapped. "By your account, I'm not even a priestess."

She inclined her head, granting a point where it was due. "There was a reason for the temple, child. A good one. Priestesses feed on energy," she said, and took a step around the edge of her desk. Breaking the pendulum pattern we'd fallen into. "It sustains us. Gives us great reserves with which we are tasked to offer aid. Comfort to the dying. Healing for those who might be saved. But we never," she murmured, "take without restraint. Never too much from any one thing. There are rules that guide us. Protections set in place thousands of years before I was born—"

"To keep you from becoming me," I guessed, breath coming hard as she moved to sit at the edge of her desk. Closer, but making no effort to touch.

"Empaths are dangerous," Sasha agreed, folding her hands before her once more. "They've no training to protect them. Nothing but a legendary hunger to feed on energy. Forgoing food, they take sustenance from the energy around them. Unable to stop, they become slaves to that thirst. Killing at will, utterly absent discretion. That you're alive at all is an incredible stroke of good fortune, for while the legends differ on how, they all have the exact same roots. An empath escapes training in the temple, matures without guidance, and kills hundreds before she is put down by those who might have been sisters."

I shivered, but it wasn't the freezing burn of hatred pumping through my veins—it was fear. A whisper of something *other* lingering just out of reach. But I forced it back, and said, "So priestesses *can* use their gifts for war."

"Priestesses can do a lot of things," she hedged. "None of them available to *you*."

"So, what?" I laughed, clipped low and bitter. "You mean for me to accept my fate as a slave. Let him use me to kill?" Head shaking, I set my feet, sweating and trembling. Reeking of spent seed and stolen innocence. "I won't do it. If you won't help me, I'll find a way to kill him myself."

At this, Sasha stood. Touching my wrist with fingers that were cool and soothing. "I can only presume your time spent in the forest—*alone*—is what kept you from succumbing to the curse of an empath. And now?" she said, and I blinked. Slow and drowsy. "In the middle of a war, surrounded by power and death? It can only be your bond with the young captain."

I took a breath, matching her steady inhale. "Why?"

"You're an empath, Mila," she said again, thumb

stroking over my heated flesh. "You need a counter-balance. A shield between you and the world you'll be driven to consume. Asher is that correction. The elite to your priestess." A serene smile spread across her lips. One I couldn't help but match. "Where we feed, they purge. Expending more energy than they possess, it was rare for them to live beyond their twenties before the advances in technology."

"Before they conquered Tritan inside of a week," I said, but the sentiment lacked the cutting edge of bitter resentment.

She shrugged. "You cannot kill him without also killing yourself. Not now, and probably not before."

Searing hurt saw me lurch away from the sedative in her touch. "My death means nothing if he dies with me," I snapped. "The captain will pay for what he did to me. What he's done."

For a moment, Sasha simply watched me tremble. And then, "What did he do?"

I sneered, turning so she couldn't see. Couldn't feel the writhing hurt.

The skin of my inner thighs pulled where they rubbed. Chafing where they'd grown tacky with drying sperm.

"I won't do anything that helps him kill," I said instead. Fists clenched at my sides, bruised shoulder throbbing in time with my temper. "I absolutely refuse."

"You're no good to anyone dead."

"And the alternative is *what*? Offer comfort to those he kills as they lay dying when I could slaughter elites without discretion *but you won't tell me how?*" Darkness swirled at my peripherals, my stomach snarling a deep, primal hunger that needed to be fed. I scoffed, spittle misting the air between us. "You've never even seen an empath before. You've no *idea* if these so-called legends hold a whisper of truth, and no notion of what training me might look like. If it's even possible."

A smirk creased her lips, then. "And who," she asked, "do you think might tell him it's safe to use your power, should we be successful here? Who's the closest thing anyone has to an authority on priestesses *or* empaths, if not me?"

I sucked a breath between my teeth, every drop of my attention shifting to her face.

"Empaths are dangerous. Volatile," she murmured, a low, wicked timber entering her voice. "A perfect weapon for an elite—especially one like Captain Rawlings who likes to push boundaries. But without absolute confirmation that it's safe to do so, neither he nor the general will be willing to risk such an asset. Of which there is only one. And who knows?" she drawled. "It might take *years* to complete your training."

10

———

"Clear your mind," Sasha said, her voice a dull, droning hum. Sending a barb of that soothing energy through my palms, where she held my hands in hers. "Focus on this."

Taking a breath, I let myself drift. Soothed by the sound of her voice. By her energy, weak though it was—smothered and enslaved by General Tilcot and the chains buried deep in her flesh. "What are you doing?" I asked, drowsy. Complacent and calm.

She pulled at the dark flames seething behind my ribs, wrapping them in a blanket. A shroud of comforting frost that tempered the fires and eased the ache gnawing on my sinew. "Protection," she murmured. "I'm giving you a shield."

"Like th' ones the rebels made," I slurred, remembering the electric blue shimmer that tasted like hope

—until the Caledonians gobbled it up and swallowed it whole.

Sasha hummed, seeming not to understand. "I'm building something you can use to keep yourself separate from the hunger."

"Mmm not hungry," I returned, and my eyes drifted closed on a blink that grew long and heavy.

"Yes," she murmured. "But feeding on nothing but Asher's energy will only drive your thirst for more."

My heart lurched. Eyes snapping open as a bubble of fury resurfaced in an instant, my ire provoked. Overwhelming the flimsy barrier of priestess energy before she could finish her task. "I don't want more," I hissed. "I want to see him on his knees. Made to crawl"—I shivered, fingers growing tight around those that were frail and dry—"to beg."

A crease flickered between Sasha's brows, her forehead misted with a fine layer of dew. "You have to let your anger go, Mila. Learn to bend before you break."

Pressure pounded at my temples, lodged in the soft spot beneath my jaw, where it reached for my heart with barbed hooks. Taking root. *Festering.* "Why?" I spat, my breaths coming short and ragged. Jaw flexing as I ground my molars together. "Why am I the one who has to bend?"

"Because you can't beat him," she replied.

Unblinking, her icy blue stare boring into mine. "You have no power, child. No talent or skill. *Nothing.*"

Breath frozen in my chest, I felt something churn deep inside my heart. Seething where it smoldered, frothed and furious, dangling on the edge of something dangerous. Awoken for the first time. "Nothing?" I whispered, vision growing dark about the edges. Narrowed down to two points of taunting chips of ice, blind to everything else.

"You're no priestess," she pressed, pupils little more than tiny pricks of black in an ocean of blue. "Not trained to use the gifts that might have saved us. You're a plaything. Bound to service an elite."

Sweat dropped from her hairline.

Tracing down the side of her face, where it was caught in fine lines. Growing larger as it fell, absorbing the anxious moisture gathered on pale skin.

I exhaled through clenched teeth. Her words worming through my flesh and bone, burrowing into the fat. Feasting on greasy suet in such a way that left me breathless and dizzy.

"Just another tool of war for the empire to use," she continued. "So much potential, gone to waste. Used in the fight against her own people. Who was it that kept you from the temple?" she asked, panting now. Her cheeks glowing with heat, despite the way her eyes chilled me to the core. "Such arrogance could only be the doings of a man. Was it your father?" A short, breathless laugh bounced off my cheeks. My lips. And she said, "Ah, yes," through a sneer that didn't suit her genteel features. "It was. I can feel the way it hurts you to admit it. But you know it's true."

"Stop," I gasped, the syllable hardly bothering to cross my clenched teeth. My knuckles bloodless where they were locked around Sasha's fingers. And just there, splashing at the back of my throat —*burning*—a cauldron of pure, seething rage begging to be loosed. A beast over which I had no control.

She grinned, then. Cruel and wicked, a sharp thing designed to provoke. "It was your father who left you unprotected, Mila. He all but gifted you to the Caledonians. Ensured you'd be passed around between them, fought over until there's nothing left but an empty, obedient vessel. A slave. Soiled... *used...*"

Acid boiled over as I stared into her eyes and saw nothing.

Just another betrayer.

A traitor who promised help but offered only pain.

Embracing the way it burned as it spattered over my lips, I did the only thing I could.

I unleashed the storm...

... and crashed into a wall of pure white energy.

A shield.

Tinged with electric blue.

My knees buckled, sending me crashing to the floor in a boneless heap. Both wrists caught in a frigid vice of bone and ice.

"The elites were born and bred for war," she said, standing strong. Unbent. Towering above me as power billowed all around her. "But it is only a priestess who can take something corrupt and make it something new."

And then I knew.

What she'd done.

Why she'd provoked me into violence.

It was *my* energy she wielded. Dark flames tempered by a master—a woman who needed no power of her own to see me beaten.

Vision going blurry, I took a breath. The first one I could recall that *wasn't* bogged down by the weight of failure and shame. A breath that didn't stink of poisonous elite energy. It was fresh and crisp. The closest I might ever come to freedom.

"Thank you," I whispered, and felt the scalding heat of tears when they spilled over my lashes. "I don't—"

"A shield won't save you," she said, and released my wrists. Cupping my face in both palms, her thumbs traced over the wetness on my cheeks. "But it's a start. Something for us to build a solid foundation upon."

I nodded, chin dipping as her hands fell away. Unable to bring myself to stand, I dragged my knees to my chest instead. Curling around myself so I might prod at the thing she'd built and stare in helpless wonder.

The beast, too, was held rapt and enthralled.

A tentative knock rapped at the door. "Priestess?"

"Come in," Sasha said, and reclaimed her seat with a weary sigh I felt echoing through my own chest.

Alicia peeked through a crack in the door. "You're needed in the infirmary."

Sasha rubbed the bridge of her nose between forefinger and thumb. "Thank you, Alicia. I'll be out in a moment. We're just finishing up."

The door snapped shut.

I didn't look up from where my ankles were crossed, when I said, "Am I going to get pregnant?"

For a long moment, my question went unanswered. I was left to sit in an uncomfortable silence. One that only grew heavier with every passing second.

And then, "No," Sasha said, and stood. Turning, she uncovered a glass case containing the unmistakable glitter of gold. An unused set of chains matching those that were sunk into her flesh and mine. "It's the chains. Once activated, they interfere with our natural cycles. The bound priestesses are infertile."

I nodded, swallowing a hard lump, but that was it.

Moving to stand before me, she extended her hand, and said, "You did well today, Mila."

Taking her hand without meeting her eye, I snorted. Knowing it wasn't true. I hadn't done anything but react, take the bait she'd laid before me, and reveal myself to be exactly what she thought me to be.

Dangerous.

Volatile.

An empath.

"I'll see you soon," she murmured, one hand on the door. The other on my lower back.

"Tomorrow?" I asked, and cringed. Hating the eager lilt to my voice, yet unable to pretend it was a lie.

She shrugged. "Unless something comes up." A tiny, sad smile flickered at the edge of her lips. "Such is the life of a slave."

I shuddered, rolling my neck—and bumped the crescent bruises left high on my shoulder. But instead of leaning into the pit of seething hatred, I reached instead for the glimmering shield built by an artist. Drinking it in, I bathed my dampened senses in a wash of cool strength before I turned to go.

Centered. Refreshed.

It wasn't much, as far as plans went, but it was a start. Something that didn't belong to the captain or the empire. Something shared between women who might one day be equals.

11

"Ready to go, wildcat?" Marco asked, falling into step at my right, leaving Gabe to guard my back.

Pretending I didn't notice Alicia's absence, I held my chin high. Said nothing as they guided me through the ornate halls of the general's manse.

Gabe chuckled. "Told you. Girl's got a Marco filter. Just picked it up faster than most."

"Not possible," Marco returned. "At the very most, she's just worn out from a day of training with Sasha. But"—he grinned—"it's far more likely that the lady wildcat is just intimidated by my dashing good looks."

We exited the manse to find a city consumed by darkness. Hours had passed in training with Sasha— in a windowless room—without my being able to take note, the entire day spent free of the captain... despite what had grown tacky and sour as it dried.

An ever-present reminder I could not escape.

Just as he wanted.

I shuddered, disgusted and ashamed. Taking small, mincing steps that kept my thighs together, the scent of stale semen trapped beneath the billowing layers of my skirts.

"Hold on there, priestess," Gabe said, and set a restraining hand on my shoulder. "Can't go rushing on without us. Captain's orders."

Frowning, I shook off his touch and turned my attention in, to touch that shining buffer of pure energy. Braced for the coming fight. To face the man who'd left me in ruins, who'd taken something precious and made it his own.

The streets were dark.

The air damp with the onset of night.

All around me the scent of distrust lingered at the back of my sinuses. Thick and cloying, an ominous weight that hung on the breeze as the soldiers scanned the streets for any hint of danger.

But I closed my eyes to all of it, feet silent on the cobbles as I followed without complaint. Too tired to do more than obey, I was enthralled by what Sasha had given me. Charmed, pacified by a thing of beauty no one else could see.

A thing that would ensure a measure of distance remained between me and the captain's lewd intentions. A wall of protection granted by the Head Priestess herself.

And when the captain's residence loomed dark and ominous at the end of the street, I dared a tiny, secret smile.

Things would be different this time. This time, he wasn't facing some terrified, untouched innocent.

There was nothing left to lose. A *new* barrier between us that couldn't be breached by mere flesh.

In the least traditional sense, I was armed.

Keeping me sandwiched between them, Marco and Gabe entered without hesitation and guided me through gloomy halls. And even in the dark, I recognized the way to the captain's office. Knew the place where he'd first put me on my knees and introduced me to the monster lurking beneath the handsome veneer.

At the sound of a throaty, feminine chuckle, the soldiers paused. Content to wait in the hall until summoned.

"Well it was *your* slave who ruined dinner, after all," she said. "I think the least you can do is treat me to a proper meal."

The low murmur of the captain's voice answered her, unintelligible at such a low pitch.

I frowned, glancing at Marco.

"Carina," the soldier supplied, and didn't bother to hide the exasperated roll of his eyes.

Teeth clenched, I nodded. Eyes adjusting to the low lighting as we stood in wait.

Silent.

Made to listen to the one-sided conversation until Carina said, "Mmm, well I have nowhere to be, Asher. I could stay for just... a little longer." She giggled, and I turned my attention to the shield. Letting that soothing power wash my senses clean before I was forced to endure a Caledonian courtship in real time. "I could stay all night..."

But a few seconds later, the door swung open. Blinding us with a warm, yellow glow as Carina stumbled out, awash in a cloud of alcoholic fumes. Her elegance left rumpled and askew, the fine coil of dark hair mussed as if straightened in haste and without a mirror. And at the corner of wine-stained lips, a smudge of makeup and blurry lines.

It took a moment, but when she realized she wasn't alone, her reaction was not one of shameful contrition, but instant haughty contempt. "What a surprise," she slurred, taking a single step toward me. "Should have known I'd find Asher's little pet lurking in the dark. Listening. I sure hope you learned something valuable," she cooed, and jabbed a perfectly shaped fingernail into my chest. "Perhaps you need instruction, hmm?"

I said nothing. Offered her nothing but a slow blink. Distracted from my meditation by the lancing sparkle of pain as she scored my breastbone. And then her fingers glided up, to pinch at either side of my jaw, to hold me in place so she might watch and see the impact her words held as they struck my ears.

"He may be bound to you," she breathed, stinging my eyes with the flammable quality of her breath, "but it'll be *my* bed he seeks when we're married. I'll see to it. That you're allowed to watch. To clean up the mess." She smirked, smoothed her hair back into place, and adjusted her rumpled skirts. "Foreign pussy may be an entertaining distraction, but it takes one of his own kind to truly satisfy a man like *that*."

It happened in an instant.

In one breath, I was existing inside myself. Content to brush against the pure, numbing bliss that was my shield.

In the next, I lashed out. Using the cruel touch clamped tight about my jaw, I dove straight into the Caledonian woman towering above me. Flooding through her system, I mimicked what Sasha had done to me. Flush with excess, I was seduced by Carina's unstable energy, meek an unappetizing as it was.

Mundane.

Almost indiscernible, it was utterly void of the intoxicating crackle of dark, elite flames. Bland and tasteless next to the wash of soothing, complex might of a priestess.

I felt the bruise still smarting on Carina's shin and knew a brief flash of spiteful pride for having been the one to inspire it.

I swam through veins swollen with drink, explored old injuries, and grew intimate with a woman whose heart floundered at the thought of the man I hated most in the world.

All before Marco took his next blink. Before either soldier could do more than part their lips in my defense, I spun through her system and loosed the dark thing slavering for a taste.

A creature Sasha had provoked only to cage. Primed for battle, then denied.

The empath.

Newborn. Clumsy and curious, it pulsed from my skin into hers. Messy. Wreaking delightful havoc.

I drank her in. Watched her pupils balloon wide as a delicious tendril of fear spiked through her brainstem. Pulling at everything that went unseen, I took what little she had and made it my own. Patching the holes the captain had left behind with the vitality of his intended bride.

She staggered.

"Easy now," Gabe said, and caught the fragile woman before she hit the floor. "Let's get you home, eh?"

Panting through gaping lips, I blinked. Nipples tiny, beaded points that strained against the fabric of my silken dress. Sweat dotting all along my hairline as my vision grew swampy with a distorted haze, as the contact between us was broken and Gabe escorted the drunkard away from my presence.

I swayed, tongue thick and tacky inside my mouth. Cheeks flushed, my brain swollen, pressed tight against the inside of my skull in such a way that made my neck ache with the effort to keep myself upright.

Spinning and wobbly.

A rough hand settled on my shoulder blade.

Marco.

His identity flashed behind my eyes without my having to look, but was gone before I could reach for more.

Feet moving, I stumbled into the captain's office at Marco's insistence—and faltered when I saw a familiar head of ebon-black hair. Forehead resting on steepled fingers, the captain was dressed in the same clothing he'd been wearing when I'd seen him last.

But now he was rumpled. Disheveled.

His hair mussed, sticking out at odd angles.

Marco cleared his throat, drawing that inky gaze up to reveal bloodshot eyes both glassy and unfocused.

"Carina is a..." Marco trailed off, pausing to pull out a chair and fold himself into it, leaving me idle and swaying in the background, excluded at the fringe of their private chat. "She's an... *interesting* choice for marriage, sir."

The captain snorted, running long fingers through his hair. "She's a toxic whore," he said, "but she's got good breeding." Scrubbing one palm down his face, he scratched at his stubble then poured himself another drink. "Haven't decided if I want to accept her proposal just yet."

Marco snatched the glass of amber liquid, draining it in two messy swallows. "Seems eager enough. Comes with more than a few beneficial political connections."

"Yeah," the captain said, and set his lips directly to the decanter. "And it'll tie me to the Savoy's for the rest of time." Tilting his head back, the captain drank. His throat bobbing as he worked, eyes drifting closed. Tight at the edges as if the mere thought of Carina left him in pain.

Wincing, Marco set both elbows to his knees and watched, waiting until the other took a ragged breath and cradled the bottle to his chest, before he said, "That wouldn't be *so* bad, would it? Least the view is nice."

"I'm too fuckin' drunk for this." The captain blew a noisy breath through his nose. "Or maybe I'm not drunk *enough*. Anything to report from the manse?"

Marco shook his head. "Aside from getting turned down by Alicia more times than I can count, it was quiet all day. No sign of Tilcot."

Nodding, the captain set his bottle aside and placed both palms flat on the table. Fingers spread, he took a breath, then stood. "Won't last. He'll make a move. Just gotta be ready for it."

"But a night off is nothin' to sneer at," Marco

concluded, before he too was on his feet. "Have sweet dreams, old man."

"Ha," the captain drawled. "Remind me to kick your ass in the morning, hmm?"

Marco saluted, tapping his heels together. "Absolutely, sir. I'll be sure to book us time in the fighting pits. Right at the ass crack of dawn, so we can get a solid workout in before the day begins. Nothing better to cure a hangover."

Squinting through bleary eyes, the captain chuckled. "You'll need every unfair advantage you can get, boy. Mila, come," the captain barked, and clapped one hand on the soldier's shoulder before he exited the office.

I cursed, staggering along behind him on unsteady feet. Head sloshing about inside my skull, seized by his influence, I was given no choice but to obey. Was too disoriented from the rush of Carina's boozy energy to fight.

Toxic, indeed.

Tasting her had left me without a tether. My senses dulled, swirling around my skull in a fog that tingled where it spread. Tongue tacked to the roof of my mouth, I was parched. Thirsty enough to demand, "Water," and reach for the back of the captain's shirt. "I'm thirsty."

He hummed, fisting the railing as he stumbled up the stairs, turned a sharp corner, and clipped the door frame with the edge of his shoulder.

"Come'ere," he slurred, flicking his fingers before my face. Grinning when my wrists and throat burned at his command—a dim glow lighting the gloom—he entered his private bath and kept me close. Even when he flipped the latch on his belt, shimmied where I couldn't see, and emptied his bladder.

"Not exactly what I had in mind," I drawled, cheeks flushed, scandalized, but unable to tear my attention from so intimate an experience.

A sinister gleam entered his gaze as inky eyes slid over his shoulder, but without a word, he reached for the tap at the sink and flipped it on. "Drink," he said, and shook himself off.

All but dunking my head, I obeyed. Gulping at the flood of cold water with a moan of purest bliss.

Rough hands traced the length of my spine, he took advantage. My position an invitation I hadn't meant to issue. "I *would* get the only priestess in the world who's untrained," he murmured, pressing a raspy kiss to the ring of bruises he'd left on my shoulder.

I shivered, hands shooting out to brace, but I slipped against the porcelain. Arching my back as he pressed against me, I hummed, flush with Carina's toxic, spinning energy. Brave and confidant, despite the predator draped over my back. "Poor, pitiable Asher," I cooed, and clenched when I felt him grow thick with interest. "What a tragedy for you. Such hardship."

A grin whispered at my nape—I felt it twitch. "Mmhmm," he purred, and let his pants drop to the floor. "And growing harder by the moment."

"Go bother your intended wife," I returned, knocking a jar to the floor when my head spun. The world tilting off its axis in such a way that left me clinging to the sink. Inhibitions washed away by the sloppy rush of intoxication I'd pulled from Carina's body into mine.

He tugged at the ties keeping my dress in place. "Would you like that? Watching me bed another woman?" Shifting my hair to one side, he hauled me upright. Spun, and watched with a wicked glimmer as my dress fell, pooling in a puddle at my feet. As I was exposed. My nipples already pebbled. "Or," he murmured, and sucked a breath between his teeth, "maybe you're jealous?"

I laughed through a sneer, cupping my breasts in a delayed attempt to hide from that wicked gaze. Said nothing in response to such a ludicrous sentiment.

"So," he said, and stepped into the narrow shower stall at his back, dragging me in with him. "What devious little plan have you and Sasha cooked up, hmm?"

"And what makes you think—"

"I may be drunk," he drawled, and turned the tap without so much as a backward glance. "But I'm not stupid. And you know"—a spray of cold water struck his back, making him shudder as he took the brunt of the icy blast—"I'm almost eager for the challenge. I prefer a little more… *fight* in my pets."

Recognizing the devious glimmer in those glassy eyes, I raised both hands and issued a warning. "Don't you dare—"

He tipped to the side.

I screeched, coughing as glacial water washed over my face, my chest and belly. It warmed before I could muster simple speech, but still, I trembled. Cringing back in a vain attempt to evade the frigid water. Spine pressed to the tiled wall, hands cupping my nudity as I pranced in place. "You sadistic bastard!" I hissed, scowling and dripping.

Unrepentant, the captain licked his lips and produced a bar of soap, working it into a quick lather against his chest. The suds trickling over the bumps and ridges, the pebbled flesh that rippled over his chest. A lure meant to draw my eye… *lower*.

Without a word, he pressed the soap into my hands. Head tipped back as he washed, he watched me from beneath hooded eyes, but didn't touch.

It was his influence that surged through my blood, doing his bidding, exactly as he'd promised he could. Full control with an errant thought.

And yet, he did not seem to notice the shield. He moved around it as I was made to mimic his actions. Whipping the suds into a froth, scrubbing away the day's stress—the morning's stains.

I swallowed. Blinking and disoriented, latching

onto the one thing that might lead to another small victory. That he hadn't thought to plunge inside me with dark flames that could see what others could not. Taking advantage with his senses, to learn and touch with the gifts of a priestess, for he was an elite, first. A man who thought in terms of offense and force, to whom the idea of stealthy subversion was a chore.

Breath catching, I reached instead for the unsteady verve Carina had donated.

Embraced it for what it was.

The energy of a seductress.

My fingers plucked at beaded nipples, cupping and lifting all that grew heavy beneath that obsidian stare.

Pushing lower, the captain seized his cock at the root. Squeezing as he washed, he pumped that turgid flesh without a hint of shame. Knuckles going white when I was made to do the same—my veins singing with molten gold—he grunted. A breath puffed where it hissed through clenched teeth.

I panted, reckless, holding eye contact. Unable to speak as he gave himself a show.

"Show me," he breathed, and picked up a heavy rhythm. The muscles in his forearm coiled beneath the strain, his chest flexing as he moved over his length with smooth confidence. And then, with his free hand, the captain reached for the sack hanging between his legs. Tugging, massaging at that heavy purse as his wrist twisted around the knob of flesh glaring at me with an angry, reddened tip.

I shivered—and slipped one soapy finger inside. Showing him exactly what he wanted to see. Hands moving at his whim.

"Another," he rasped, faster now. Tendons corded in his neck as he stroked. Kneading as he watched with feet spread. Chin tipped back, eyes gone utterly bottomless.

And it was then, as I obeyed, adding another finger, that I knew an instant of power over this man. This impossible, infuriating Caledonian elite who would know what it was to kneel...

He grunted. Straining. "Use your thumb," he barked. "On your clit. I want to see you fuck yourself for me."

I couldn't look away. Could hardly blink as I watched the way his hand moved, enthralled by the grip. The way his forefinger and thumb encircled his shaft and twisted at the end. Entranced by the lewd squelch of bubbles foaming and white against flesh that was quickly growing purple.

"That's it," he breathed, jaw bunched tight at the corner. Fist a noisy blur.

One hand kneading my nipple, the other edging me closer to victory or complete destruction, I let my chin fall so I might watch him from beneath a curtain of silver-blonde hair.

To hide the smirk as I seized upon a rule of this

sordid game—to mirror Captain Asher Rawlings and give the visual creature exactly what he wanted.

I moaned. Like a whore. Like Carina, all confidence and stolen instinct, I spread my ankles for a better angle, and said, "Please," in a desperate, breathless sort of way that made him lurch toward me. "A-Asher," I whispered, begging through the fan of my lashes. "Please, Asher—"

"*Fuck*," he snarled, and aimed at my pumping fingers. "Don't stop. Work that clit, Mila. That's it," he groaned, and his fist stopped. Knuckles white, a pearlescent rope gushed from his tip. Splashing against my mound, coating the back of my hand in a sticky warmth I could feel even through the falling water.

He pumped again, and sent another jet to splash against my swollen flesh.

Again.

And again.

Coating my fingers in a creamy glaze, his seed made my work slippery and unfocused—enough that I was distracted when I might have fallen into ecstasy. Prevented from following him into orgasm, I turned away from the temptation of that fall and dove instead into the comforting numb that was my shield.

He took no notice.

Falling forward, one hand braced on the wall beside my cheek, he continued to milk himself dry. Breath ragged against my lips as he emptied himself against me, the captain painted my pussy. Eyes glassy as he tainted that obscene canvas.

It wasn't until his fist came to a slow stop that he frowned at my still fingers. Ebon eyes flicking up, glazed and suspicious, he found my lips stretched over a smug smile.

I said nothing.

Merely existed behind the shimmering wall of insulation that kept us separate. Working instead to calm my racing heart. To ignore the throbbing, empty ache where his seed marked me yet again.

He snorted, then, showing off a row of straight, white teeth. "Oh, well done, Mila," he breathed. "But are you sure you want to play this game, pet?"

Serene, I lifted one shoulder in casual indifference. Refusing the bait dangling before me.

"You think denying yourself is a victory?" he purred, and looped his forearm behind my neck just to tangle his fingers in my hair. To tip my head back as he crowded in. Pressing too close, his lips moved against my cheek—his free hand moved to cup my mound. Fingers slipping through the mess of slick folds to tease and circle. "You think"—he ground the heel of his palm against my clit, smearing himself all over me—"it hurts my pride to know you haven't peaked, is that it?"

Two rough fingers plunged inside, stuffing his come inside me, and I choked on a gasp. Tenuous grip on my shield rocked, but held in place.

"I *like* knowing you've been left on the edge," he confided, and nibbled at my ear. Sucked and pinched. "That you'll spend the night aching and ripe. My cock filling your dreams the way it won't fill this greedy..." He sent a careful tendril of energy straight into my core, grinning when I squealed and twisted. "... *needy*..." A throbbing pulse bloomed behind my pelvic bone, everything south of my bellybutton growing taut with tension. "... *desperate* little cunt."

He pulled back with speed enough to leave me reeling. Clenching around nothing, left hanging on the cusp of a truly powerful release, he forced my every muscle to still. Kept me frozen, lips gaping around a silent scream as the drive to seek my climax was diverted.

Cut off.

A tormented, desperate sound crackled over my lips. But that was all.

Cruelty etched deep into the lines on his face, he swept his fingers through the mess of clotted cream cooling against my flesh. "Taste it before you swallow," he murmured, and fed me the very same digits that had driven me to humiliation so quickly. With the sort of expertise I could never hope to match.

Salty and strong, the captain's brine wrinkled my nose—but I swallowed him down.

"Good girl," he cooed, and shut off the water. Stooped, and hauled me off my feet.

I clung to naked flesh as he walked, trembling

with fatigue. My senses reeling and overwrought. Teased by a victory only to lose it in an instant.

Aching to be filled—to be *fucked*, hard and rough and filthy—by the man I hated most.

He tossed me onto the bed, laughing at my wordless squeal, and was on me before I could even attempt to retreat. Straddling my hips, he pinned me to the sheets. Both of us wet. Skin prickling. Too hot.

And then he guided my wrists up, securing both above my head before he dipped to pull my nipple into the searing heat of his mouth.

"Please," I whimpered, and my thighs fell apart. An invitation I didn't mean to give but couldn't take back. Not with the phantom of Carina's energy in the bed between us. Not when his hips notched into place and he swapped one beaded tip for the other.

A click ratcheted into place. Twin bands of cold steel banded about my wrists.

Handcuffs.

Affixed to his bed frame.

"Sweet dreams, little empath," he whispered—and abandoned me in a puddle of shameful wet. Pussy weeping for just a *hint* of attention. A tiny push that might offer relief, a sip of mercy now that his point was well and truly made.

Instead, he pulled the covers back and flicked them over us both. Rolling to his stomach, one arm disappeared beneath a pillow.

He fell asleep with a smirk set to his lips. Naked, hair tousled, curling at the ends as it dried.

I watched the moon pass across dimpled glass, and when I did manage to claim sleep, my dreams were anything but sweet.

12

dull, thumping ache throbbed in my temples as sunlight warmed my eyelids. Insulting in its intensity.

I squinted against the offense, pressing my face deeper into the pillow and exhaled.

Horrible breath bounced back in my face.

Teeth coated in a fuzzy layer, I swallowed and tasted something foul. Groaning, too hot, I tried to roll and was caught up by the handcuffs binding my wrists. By a weight draped over my hip. My ribs.

Asher.

Wrapped all around me, he slept. Oblivious, his left hand cupping my breast, his front aligned with my back, he was hard.

Achingly so.

Twitching where he was pressed against the curve

of my bottom, I could feel a drop of wetness both slimy and sticky pooled against my skin.

And before I could choke it down, I whimpered. Hypersensitive, sopping wet from a sleepless night of torment, my eyes *burned* with exhaustion. And my stomach—roiling and empty—snarled. Twisting around nothing, screaming to be filled only half as loud as the need to feel that thick length spearing into me—

Teeth clenched, I tried to reach for my shield and found a wall of elite energy instead.

Banked and sleepy... a veritable buffet of dark flames ripe for the picking.

Salivating, I pressed into him. Back flexing, I pulled at his essence. Just a sip... a single... harmless taste to dispel my appetite before I begged him for something to eat...

I rolled my neck, face pressed into the pillow to drown my sigh as I reached for the burn and found it sweet.

An ambrosia that grew all the sweeter with every passing second, until I couldn't stop.

Drinking in a single, unending gulp that bypassed the empty pit in my stomach, I gorged myself on all things Asher.

He sucked in a stuttering breath.

Stretched.

Groaned.

Squeezing that handful of fat and flesh, he rolled

my nipple, then wormed his free hand between us to take himself in hand. Nudging my thighs apart, he sent his length sliding through sodden lips. Lubricated by an easy glide, he thrust through my folds with a lazy roll of his hips. The tip of his cock teasing my clit when it sluiced through sodden heat, and peaked through to the other side.

Fists clenched, I tried to tip my pelvis down. To catch the head of his cock where I ached the most and take him inside.

Mumbled words vibrated against my nape. "Slept well?"

I lurched away from the sound of his voice. The smug cruelty that lapped at my shoulder and flickered through my chest.

"Mmm, don't stop on my account," he drawled. Following my retreat with one hand heavy on my hip. His prick still lodged between my thighs, I could feel his heartbeat throbbing at my core.

I didn't think.

Couldn't.

I reacted.

Hurling a barb, I launched an attack. Clumsy and faltering, I wormed my way deeper. Ravenous, hurting and depleted, I tried to feast on my elite. Tried to leave him drained and weak.

Helpless.

Just as he'd left me.

And so I felt it when he came fully awake. When

he went still at my back, letting me take my fill. Above all... curious to see where this might lead.

I felt it all.

Every flickering emotion. Each and every one of his aches and pains.

Everything.

Groaning, he rolled, spread my thighs and draped my left knee over his hip, settling above me. Looming on the edge of action, he chose instead watch me with pupils blown wide as they might go. Hot and thick, but restrained, inky eyes fixed not to my nipples, but to my face. Sober now, I felt it when his curiosity became full-blown interest.

Wrists pressing into the cold bite of steel, I hiccuped. Straining against my restraints, I grew sloppy and unfocused as I neared the limit of what I could take.

"My turn," he whispered, and showed me what an elite really was.

Pushing, he sent a bolt of energy through my skin.

The elite to my priestess, *he* fed *me.* Expelling massive quantities of pure, dark magic with a control that put my paltry attempt to shame.

Everywhere he touched, electrified. Ribs, nipples, stomach, he held himself aloft and let one hand wander. Caressing, his fingertips left corruption in their wake.

"I know you can feel it," he murmured, and nudged at my entrance. Blunt and heavy, his tip sent lightning racing through my blood. Made me arch and mewl, shame heating my skin in such a way that I couldn't help but succumb to it. "I know you can feel what you do to me. But let's see," he whispered, and flashed a devious grin, "what my sexy little vixen needs, hmm?"

I shook my head, but that was all I could muster before he turned the tide. Before he unleashed the opposite end of the spectrum and hit me with a wave of my own making.

Priestess magic.

What he held no rights to, but wielded as if he'd been trained by the Head Priestess herself.

Racing through my blood, he tasted and took. Feeding. Muscles trembling as he held himself in check, restrained, he showed me what control *really* was.

And then he struck my shield.

"Ah," he breathed, forehead dipping to bump against mine. "So this is what Sasha's been teaching you, hmm?"

"N-no," I whispered, eyes drifting shut on the denial I knew he could feel before it even crossed my lips.

He slipped one hand beneath my lower back, spread his fingers against the base of my spine, then pulled my hips into him. Grinding against the flood of wet heat, he tormented me with a surge of male arousal—both inside and out. The underside of his thick cock slid against my clit, throbbing where he was poised to claim. And when I tried to twist away, he sent heated blood to swell tissue already weeping for release.

"No?" he whispered, and pressed a kiss to my collarbone. "Come now, Mila. You can do better than that. Fight me, pet. Show me the brave warrior priestess whose greedy little pussy woke me up with such a ferocious need."

"That's not"—I shivered—"that's not what happened."

He laughed. "Ah, yes. I forgot. This is all me, isn't it? All my fault."

Straining, my stomach grew taut. Concave, *hollow* as I curled around myself—toward *him.*

"I'll admit, it's quite something," he mused, assaulting me with a bolt of pure, unfiltered lust. Prodding at the shield as if it were nothing to do so. To split himself in two and leave me in ruins. "Ingenious, really. But what's it for?"

I blinked. Trembling, my skin slick with arousal and sweat. Asher held me in thrall and filled me with a sense of overwhelming compliance. "It's a shield," I whispered, caught in the bottomless pools of inky black. Ensnared somewhere too deep to name, my lips loosened.

Forcing my neck to bend, he pressed a kiss to the hollow at the base of my throat. "Mmhmm."

"For protection. To"—I panted, licking at the

points of my teeth and wet parched lips—"to keep me separate from... from the hunger. The thirst for... *more*."

Teeth dragged along the tight lines bunched and corded down the length of my throat. "The empath."

"*Yesss*," I hissed, squirming against his heat. "I'm not... not a priestess. 'M nothing. *Nothing*. Can't win with no power. No talent... no..." I gasped, and tried to pull my wrists free from the handcuffs. "No skills. Daddy wouldn't—he said—he said the temple was for commoners who had no options. No connections. That I would be wasted in a life of worship... But now"—I hiccuped around a sob—"I'm a tool of war. To be passed around. Fought over. *Used*. A-and not even the shield can save me," I rasped, shaking some- where deep inside, where a crack had become a canyon.

For the space of several long breaths, the captain merely continued to run his lips along my flesh. Leaving me to tremble beneath him. Overcome by a torrent of emotions I hadn't known were there.

Grief I would never have voiced had he not mucked about inside my head... cracked open my heart.

A soft knock at the door shattered the moment, and in one fluid motion, he unlocked my handcuffs, rolled, and stepped into a rumpled pair of pants. "Come in," he called, not bothering to find himself a shirt.

Reeling, I stayed where I'd been abandoned. Spread and exposed. The sheets tangled about my nudity serving only to paint a picture of what had transpired here.

It was Alicia.

It was *always* Alicia.

"Breakfast!" she chirped, hands laden with a tray of food piled high. Her cheeks over-bright as she arranged her delivery on the captain's desk without glancing in my direction. "Is there anything else you need, sir?"

"We're headed to the bathhouse today," the captain returned, hopping to adjust his pant—where he was swollen enough to take extra care with the zipper. "See that one of the private baths is prepared?"

She inclined her head, said, "Of course," and left without another word. Rushing off to please her master in a swirl of skirts and lingering perfume.

Plucking a folded square from the top of the pile, the captain's eyes flicked over a note. His brow drawn and bunched by the time he said down, he scowled at the fruit as if it had personally offended him.

But through a thunderous scowl, he said, "Hungry?" and tucked into the platter.

I swallowed, struggling to force myself upright for the feeling of being too full. Bloated not in body, but in spirit. Elite energy sloshing around in my head.

"Come," he drawled, and flicked a serviette open.

"Eat. It would seem Sasha went to a lot of trouble to feed you something other than my energy." With a sneer, he crumpled the note and tossed it aside.

Dizzy, I staggered from the bed in a show of naked, jiggling skin. Drawing the captain's attention away from his meal as I reached for the bed sheets once more. Padding over on the balls of my feet, I inhaled the scent of bacon, sausage, and an assortment of fried things that churned my stomach.

Without a word, he set two fingers to the edge of the tray and spun it, offering me a selection of fried mashed potatoes. A pile of fruit and vegetables of every type and color I hadn't seen even before the war.

My stomach rumbled in loud anticipation, and despite *everything*... I blushed.

Grinning, he brought a forkful to his lips. "Bashful, hmm?"

I rolled my eyes. Sinking into the chair opposite, one hand clutching at bunched fabric, I dug in to the first palatable meal I'd had on Caledonian soil. Seized by a sudden ravenous hunger, I ate with reckless abandon. Hardly bothering to take the time to chew before swallowing and moving on to the next mouthful.

It wasn't long before my side of the tray was picked clean—barring the wall of things left behind that had been touching charred flesh and the rinds of my feast.

I hiccuped, unable to recall a time in which I'd been so full. So... utterly sated.

And yet *aching* for something more...

"Fuck*sakes*, Mila," the captain said, already finished. A large portion of his meal left untouched. "That was impressive."

I wrinkled my nose. "Was it?"

"I've never seen a woman eat with such—" He paused to stroke at the stubble on his chin, then said, "Enthusiasm. Where could you have possibly hidden all that food? You're such a little thing."

"Yes, well." I cleared my throat. "These things are bound to happen. Especially when your all-powerful master forgets to feed you for days on end."

It was his turn to blush, and he inclined his head. Affording a point where it was due. "If you're finished," he said after a beat, and moved to stand. "I'm nursing a cankerous hangover, and"—he grimaced—"I can smell myself. It's time for a bath."

13

The bathhouse.

We were back.

To a place that held horrible memories of being exposed... the truth of my heritage revealed, where the captain had put his mark on my skin and enslaved me to his every crude whim.

It was a traditional Caledonian bathhouse, one that supported communal bathing and a full harem. Where women were *eager* for the male attention that offered a paltry sip of power in the form of coin. A place where I might have been trained for use in all my holes, where I'd be made to learn the art of seduction and feminine cooing. To be devious if it meant my own survival.

A place that wasn't my destiny, for instead, I'd been cursed with priestess blood.

Choking on a breath heavy with the scent of

perfumed creams and oils—the air nauseatingly moist and humid—I staggered. Clinging to the captain's jacket to keep myself upright as I blinked through the urge to vomit.

"It takes some getting used to," he admitted, not unkind when he laid a steadying hand on the back of my neck. Grounding me.

I shook him off, turning instead toward the harem and the large public bathing pool where the very last of my secrets had been shampooed away.

"And where exactly do you think you're going?"

Teeth bared, I didn't bother to meet his eye when I hurled a biting, "You get exactly one guess," over my shoulder.

He chuckled, low and sinister. Catching my wrist, he made me turn. "I don't bathe with the slaves, Mila. We're going upstairs. To the private baths."

I shook my head. "No. I'm not—"

"You know, it's funny," he said, and stooped. Setting his shoulder against my stomach, his left arm swept the backs of my knees and he lifted me before I could do more than squeal in protest. "But I don't recall asking what *you* wanted to do."

"Put me *down*," I hissed, hands scrambling to ensure my nudity was concealed. That the breeze caressing my nethers wasn't evidence that I'd been exposed to any who might glance our way

But he ignored me.

Taking the stairs two at a time, my weight seemed

not to bother him despite the cankerous hangover or the heat. And when he pushed open the door to a large, tiled room, he didn't so much as falter when steam billowed around his feet.

It wasn't until the sound of male laughter echoed from inside that he went stiff, the band of his forearm tightening about my thighs. Dark flames flickering hot and possessive against my ribs.

"Still haven't broken her in, eh?"

Setting me down, the captain made sure I had my feet before he turned to face the other—a face I recognized from General Tilcot's disastrous dinner. A bound elite, the very same man who'd been so jealous to learn my freedom had been worth a mere fifty dollars.

With a shrug, the captain said, "As I'm sure you've heard, the last few days have been especially... *stressful*, Colonel Viridian."

"Conrad, please," the colonel said. "I think we can forgo the appropriate designations while soaking in the nude, hmm?"

They both laughed, but when the captain's fingers found the ties of my dress, I balked. "Alright then, Conrad," he drawled, following when I tried to bolt. "It would seem I've managed to find myself a rather rare priestess." His jaw grew tight, and without giving me an inch, he pulled at my ties. Leaving me to scramble in an attempt to keep my modesty intact.

"One whose power I cannot use without dire consequences."

"Yes, that *is* the most current gossip," the colonel hummed. "What was it the general said? Off active duty until..."

A muscle jumped at the corner of the captain's jaw. "Until she's properly trained, yes."

With a chuckle, Colonel Viridian ran his hands through thick, greying hair. Slicking it back with wet hands. "Guess there's a few setbacks to bargain hunting for priestess, hmm my boy? Bet you wish you'd spent more than a measly fifty dollars."

Returning his grin, the captain's hands found my hips. Squeezing. "Perhaps," he admitted, but that was all. Everything else left unsaid, yet somehow echoing all around us with volume enough to make me blush all the way from the roots of my hair, past my collarbones, and into the bunched fabric concealing my breasts.

"Ah, very good." The colonel tipped his head back, watching through curious eyes. "Well, if you find yourself in need of assistance, reach out, will you? I'm fascinated by the tactical ramifications behind her issues. And"—he waggled bushy, silver brows—"I bet I could have her behaving inside of a week."

"That won't be necessary, sir," the captain replied. "Mila is mine to break. And we're enjoying ourselves entirely too much, aren't we pet?"

Lip curled, I sneered but held my tongue behind clenched teeth, lest he force my silence.

A deep belly laugh rumbled up from the colonel's side of the bath. "I thought as much. Feisty little thing, is she?"

"All fire and fury," the captain agreed, but the gleam in those inky eyes was for me alone. "A complete pain in my ass," he added, and my wrists and throat surged to life, igniting with the all-too familiar tingle that seized my every muscle with involuntary obedience. And with little decorum, the captain folded me into his chest. Stripped me bare. Leaving my bottom exposed to Colonel Viridian's perusal, but kept everything else for himself.

Absent a single shred of regard for his own modesty, the captain undressed. Flicking the latch on his belt, he let his pants fall. His shirt went next, pulled over his head without bothering to work the buttons loose.

"That's striking," the colonel hummed at my back. Closer than he had been a moment before, but I was unable to turn and look. My muscles thrumming with a low-grade drone of compulsion. "It's as if the gold actually runs through her veins."

The captain made a sound at the back of his throat. Wrapping me up in a band of corded muscle, he lifted me, stepped over the lip of the bath, and sank into the luxury of heated water with a gusty sigh. "I think it's linked to her disability."

"I've never seen anything quite like it," the colonel said, watching as the captain claimed a place on a submerged bench. One that left him half in, half out of the water. His torso left dry as he moved to drape me across his lap—my weight sitting heavy across his thighs, where I couldn't squirm without feeling him grow stiff beneath me. Couldn't press for distance without exposing myself to the colonel.

And so I sat.

Curled into the arms of the man I hated most, seeking protection in a prison. My cheeks flushed with mortified heat. Jaw clenched tight enough to feel an answering throb echo in my temples.

Tormented.

"Have you any leads into what might be causing these issues?" the colonel asked, and took a sip from a sweaty glass left outside of the pool. "I took a look through the state records and saw nothing that bore even a slight resemblance among any of the other priestesses."

For a moment, as the captain's fingers tightened on my hip, I thought he'd choose not to answer. And then, "Apparently I've got the only one like her," he murmured. "In several generations. Not even Sasha has seen the like. She's an 'empath', or so we've been led to believe."

The colonel frowned. "An empath, you say? Good to know. I'll ask my girl. Carly was in training to become the next Head Priestess, after all. Let's see if their stories match up."

My heart skipped, and I flicked a glance at the colonel's face. Breath caught in my chest, unsure whether or not Sasha's teachings would hold up under scrutiny—and what it would mean for *me* if it didn't.

"We wouldn't want her affliction to spread," the captain said, pressing a grin to the spot beneath my ear. "Unless," he drawled, "we can figure out some way to harness such raw potential. I presume you saw the damage I was able to unleash with a single shot?"

"I did," the colonel confirmed, pausing as if to say something else. Something... unsavory. And then, "But I wasn't the only one who took note. Me?" He clicked his tongue. "I'm nearing retirement. Content with what I've got. A wife, a robust lineage, and a pretty young thing devoted to servicing the needs my wife refuses to acknowledge," he said, and issued a wry chuckle. "But most others aren't so ready to offer support to what could be seen as a threat to their position. And the capitol? The rumblings of their interest concern me most of all."

Swallowing, the captain offered a single, tight nod that bumped my shoulder. "I hear you."

"There's to be a demonstration for the new generation of elites," he went on. "A display of power from a bound pair. A promise of what the youths might aspire to, one day. And I'm already hearing whispers,

Asher. Whispers that *you* should be the one to lead the demonstration. Not the general."

The captain's breath caught, and I felt the surge of alarm when it filtered through his blood.

"I'll help in any way I can," the colonel continued. "Be it training or research. But keep your nose clean, son. Stay low. Avoid drawing too much attention to the girl, or you may find the capitol has a sudden need for bound elites and their priestesses, if you catch my meaning."

"I do," the captain said. His tone flat. Ominous as a moment of understanding passed between them, soaring directly over my head in such a way that left me aching to ask. Curious to the point of physical pain.

Clapping pruney fingers, the colonel's lips curled around a benign smile. "Well," he said, and stood without regard to his nudity. Shocking me utterly still with the full-frontal show. The subtle, yet obvious differences between them—the only two men I'd ever had a chance to really look at. One in his prime, the other cresting the hill of middle age. "If you'll excuse me. I've some work to do. A few errands to run." He winked. "Enjoy your slave, Asher," he said, stepping from the bath in a shower of sloshing water.

We watched him leave. Silent as he toweled off, the captain's hands still, yet humming with the sort of tension that needed to break. I could feel it lurking *just there*. Below the surface.

And then we were alone.

I was alone.

Settled on the lap of a man who could counter me at every turn, with an ease that was argument enough against trying again. A hopeless endeavor.

The captain unseated me. Pushing me to stand before him in warm water that was deep enough to tease the underside of my breasts. Arms laid out across the tiles, he spread his knees, tilted his chin back, and said, "Come."

Cupping my breasts to keep them hidden, I curled my lip. Eyes flicking toward the door, cracked open enough to reveal the hallway beyond.

"Try it," the captain cooed, his eyes sparkling. Positively slavering for the hunt.

Just to be contrary, I obeyed without the use of force. My outer thighs brushing the prickle that lay between his. Forearms crossed, nipples secreted away, I drew close enough that he could touch if the urge struck, and said, "What."

It wasn't a question. The single syllable bitten off between the click of my modified canines.

"I'd like to continue our conversation," he drawled. Fingers drawing tight circles across the water's surface, where they dangled from the edge of the pool.

I swallowed, eyes flicking again to the exit. "What conversation?"

"Your shield, Mila." He licked his lips. "Tell me everything."

Tearing my gaze from that which was bottomless and beguiling, I swallowed back the vitriol. "I already did."

"Then tell me again."

Scowling, my nails bit into the meat of my palm.

"Priestesses take," he murmured, fingers twirling through the water when I refused to speak. "They feed on energy. But for you it's different, yes? More complicated."

I swallowed, glaring at the tiny whirlpools he sent toward me.

"As I understand it, this... shield Sasha built for you is meant to keep you separate from the hunger. A barrier between you and the empath. But what if there was another way? An easier way to learn control."

My gaze flicked up to meet his. Intrigued. And, head tilting, I asked, "What would you know of training a priestess that Sasha doesn't?"

Instead of responding, he peeled my fingers free of my breast. Setting dark eyes to a pink ring of irritated flesh, where the handcuffs had left me with slight bruises encircling my wrist. Above his golden mark. And then, as he had done to himself, the captain's energy filled me in a rush. The edges smoothed, dark flames almost tranquil where they lapped at broken capillaries and made them whole. Healing me from the inside, as only a priestess could.

A priestess... and *Asher.*

Cold realization washed over my nape as the skin grew pale before my eyes. Unblemished and whole. "That's how you do it," I breathed, eyes wide. Forgetting my nudity in favor of inspecting what he'd done.

He shrugged. "We're of the same coin. Priestess and elite. Opposites of a single spectrum. Energy wielders. Destroyers and healers, both."

"And you know this?" I gasped. "*You?*"

A wry smirk creased his lips, and that hand sank beneath the surface to find a grip on my flesh. Long, elegant fingers curled were my bottom met the back of my thigh, but went no further. "Why not?"

I searched his eyes for the lie. The deception that *must* be there, lurking. Waiting for the perfect moment to strike.

I found only a mask of patience. A trap clearly set, but one I couldn't ignore for the offer of salvation. A chance to defend myself with the might of an elite, to fight the empire on a level playing field and learn from my enemy so I might destroy him from within.

"Show me," I demanded, and thrust my wrist between us. Breasts bouncing free.

He glanced at my nipples. Pulled me half a step closer. "A priestess is nothing more than an elite, really. Nothing less," he said, and sent a measured tendril of energy through my skin. Feeding me as he wove an enchantment all around me. "Frost to the fire. A closed loop that breathes *and* exhales in equal measure."

And then, pulling at my energy, he drank down every drop of priestess magic left pumping through my blood. Drained in an instant, he pinned me between his thighs when I might have sagged.

"Now you," he murmured, and caught me before I sank. Lifting me with ease, he spread my thighs and bade me to sit.

I set both palms to his chest, seeking balance. *Distance.* Felt the way his heart thumped beneath my touch with an eager flutter, and couldn't help but drift just a little closer.

Displaying an easy control, he held me in thrall without the chains. Didn't so much as blink when I returned the favor and pulled at the buffet of dark energy. Gulping down the equivalent of what he'd taken. Unable to think or stop.

"That's it," he drawled, and let his head fall back. Both hands on my hips, watching, he drew me closer still. Slid me up his thighs until I bumped against that twitching length and knew the flavor of lust.

I took.

Feasting, drawn to the most vibrant parts of him, I latched onto the piece that burned the brightest. I exhaled through parted lips, and felt my entire body go taut and lax, all at once. Tight in the middle, I melted against his chest. Lulled by the gentle lapping of tiny waves as he guided my hips in a slow grind. Teasing us both, winding me tighter as I was made to rock against that twitching length.

"Do you feel it?" he murmured, and tangled his fingers in my hair. Pressing me closer as he flexed, as he strained against me in a single, lewd thrust that spread my lips around his girth and forced that little bundle of nerves to trace him from base to tip. "It could be like this all the time. You'll never want for anything."

I frowned, confused and panting through sagging jaws.

"Let me help you, Mila," he whispered before I could protest, cupping my face so his thumbs could sweep the ridge of my cheekbones. A gentle caress that spun my fluttering heart into a knotted twist. "I can control the empath for you. Give it to me." Muscles tightening, he strained against me. Fed me another wave of aching need that left me dizzy. Enthralled. "I can ease this burden. Make it so... *so* fucking easy for you..."

Wetting my lips, I flexed my thighs. Tried to squeeze my knees together to relieve that ache.

"Take what you want," he hummed, tone a brand of seduction I couldn't ignore.

I sucked a breath through slack lips, trembling. Caught on the edge of wanting and war.

One rough hand slid down, to trace the collar embedded at my throat. Long fingers almost touching at the back of my neck. But it was the other hand that pained me, for when it slid down—weighing my breast, pausing to tweak a beaded nipple—it was to trace the length of my arm from elbow to fingertips. He collected my palm, brought my fingers to his lips, and said, "Reach for it."

A drop of sweat trickled down from my temple. And I watched when he drew my fingers between his teeth. Nibbling as those inky, gleaming eyes bored through my willpower. Every beat of my heart sending a pulse of soggy *want* to saturate my blood at his command.

"You don't need permission. Not for this," he said, and left himself wide open. Elite energy filling me without limit or boundary, he showed me the truth of that statement. "Take what you want."

And I did.

Want.

Lost to everything but the lure of what lay hidden in sable depths, I pulled my fingers from his between his teeth. Tracing the shape of his collarbone, shoulder to throat, I edged over bronzed skin to gather droplets of beaded moisture. Mesmerized by the way they fell, trickling *lower*. Over the ridges and dips of muscles I simply did not possess.

He groaned, tilting his chin back to expose his throat. To watch me from beneath a fan of dark lashes, even as he fed me a wave of virile confidence that dared me to stop.

I didn't.

Couldn't.

Not even when the hand collaring me shifted anew, when his thumb found the hollow at the base of my throat and his fingers guided my head down. To see where he jutted from the water. Red and angry and so *incredibly* swollen with need.

For me.

To touch.

Take...

Breaths coming hard, I watched a pearly drop swell at his tip. Bubbling from the tiny slit where it ached for relief.

I swallowed.

Watching my hand move, inching closer until the heel of my palm brushed flesh that lurched. Living steel.

He sucked a breath between his teeth, fingers growing tight on my nape. Silent, even as he urged me on. Driving me to be bold when I might have fled.

Wrist turning in, my fingers folded around his girth and my thumb swept up. Along a thick vein that ran down his length only to settle in the notch where his knob formed a tight *V*—just beneath the flare.

His hips bucked, and I gaped as he glided through my fist. As skin moved over his length and he strained against me, my pinky finger nestled in dark curls around the base. Where he was thicker. Where his pulse throbbed.

It was the most obscene thing I'd ever seen.

Ever *done*.

But it was his energy—raw and ravenous and electric—that made me gush. Clenching around an empty ache.

And then, with his free hand, he reached between us and wrapped his fingers around mine. Guiding me. Pumping the entire length of his shaft with long, sure strokes that twisted right at the end.

"Fuck*sakes*, Mila," he rasped, and brought my forehead to his. Bumping us together so he might look into my eyes. Trapping me there with a surge of pornographic need as we worked his cock together. And then, "Taste it," he whispered. Unblinking. Wetting his lips, his breath a surge of heat that left me panting and unable to break away.

"I-I don't—" Trembling, I shook my head, trying to clear it of the dense fog.

He nudged me back. Slid me down his thighs and back into the deepest part of the pool, moving with me as the water swallowed me up. Our foreheads still pressed together as he shifted back and spread his knees. His cock bobbing just above the surface, long and thick.

"A-Asher"—I swallowed, and released his girth as a sudden wash of terror spilled down my back—"I've never..."

Elite energy flooded my veins. Bold and pushy,

the roar loud enough in my ears that I almost didn't hear the growl that rumbled over his lips.

Instead, I followed when he sat back. When he drove me to sink into the water, one hand sweeping up to gather my hair in a loose tangle, the other tight on the back of my neck.

"Put your knees on the bench," he murmured, low and desperate. Bringing one thigh up to jut well above the surface, he made room for me to obey. To tuck me between his legs. Kneeling. Half-braced and off center, I fell forward. Hands braced on his stomach, almost weightless as I floated and knelt. "Taste it," he said again, and collected my fingers. Pulling them into the moist heat of his mouth, he sucked. Tongue laving at my digits a lewd suggestion—a direct line to the pulsing arousal weeping at my core

I couldn't help it. With a whimper, I went. One arm stretched the length of his torso, I took him in hand with the other. Let him drive me into corruption, and succumbed to the flood of elite energy.

Submerged to the tops of my thighs, my back and bottom left above the surface of steaming water, I went to all fours between his knees. The tips of my breasts hung down, teased by the swirling heat as I stared at the instrument of my destruction.

It was an instinct to tip his cock back, toward my lips. Something alien and familiar all at once, defying rational thought with a hypnotic compulsion to open for the invasion.

I didn't so much as blink.

Merely set my tongue to that flared crown and tasted the pearly bead.

Utterly consumed by the rumbling groan of a man on the edge, my heart a reckless tangle of thrashing confusion, I lapped at shining purple flesh and left him glossy.

He hissed, flexing under my command, disturbing the surface of the water in such a way that made me gape. My back arching, I panted as the waves bumped my core.

But I was already desperately wet.

Slick from something much more crude than simple water, my pussy hovered above the surface. I was tormented by gently lapping ripples that kissed those swollen, lower lips with a touch so light, so suggestive, it dragged a sob from the deepest part of me.

"That's it," he hissed, and set his thumb to my modified canines. Pulling my teeth apart as his fingers tightened in my hair. "Open for me, Mila. All the way."

Drunk on his energy, on *him*, I obeyed. Jaws sagging open, my cheeks flushed with the sort of heat I'd never known before, I let him in.

Allowing the taste of elite energy to wash away any hint of fight I might have possessed.

A breath whistled through his nose. Leaving me with the image of flared nostrils and a clenched jaw as he drove deeper into my mouth, painting the back of my tongue with a gush of salty brine.

It was a tight fit.

The shaft of his cock only *just* fitting between my canines.

And then, with the hand not tangled in my hair, he stroked the length of my spine. Nape to tailbone. Stomach curling around the crown of my head, where he had me trapped and impaled in his lap. One fist anchored in my hair to keep me pinned, he reached for my ass. Took one rounded cheek in his palm and peeled me open. Probing slick heat with long fingers, the captain sank one finger inside. Past the second knuckle.

"Just as I thought," he drawled. "Gushing for it. And to think"—he flexed his hips and sent the head of his cock deeper, nudging the back of my throat —"this was all your idea, really."

I squirmed. Taking a desperate pull of breath through my nose, tongue swirling around his head when he pulled back. The cruel drone of his words blended into a cocktail of nonsense I couldn't make sense of.

"After all," he murmured, and forced my head down until I spluttered, "it's so easy for me to infect you, isn't it?" Groaning, he added another finger. Stretching me as he worked through the mess, inching toward the back of my throat. His hand an immovable weight on the back of my head. "But this?" he asked, and pulled his fingers free with a slurp that might have made me blush if it were possible for me to be warmer without combusting. And then, lifting me off his cock by his grip on my scalp, he straightened and showed me fingers that were slick and glistening. Took himself in hand and smeared his prick with cream. "Look how your cunt weeps for me."

But he didn't let me look. Not for long. Not before he was feeding his girth between my lips once more, making me taste the tang of my own undeniable arousal as he worked my mouth over his length.

"Mmm," he groaned, and reached beneath me to pull at my nipples. First one, then the other. Fingers rolling, pinching hard enough to make me squeal when he bumped the tight ring of muscle at the back of my throat.

I choked.

"Fuck, *yes*," he hissed, and I felt him throb before he surged forward. Keeping me there, gagging around his knob as he reached and found my slit. "Did you dream of me?" he purred. "Or was it the general who made this pussy drip?"

Gagging, I couldn't so much as shake my head. Couldn't admit or deny the sordid, twisted dreams that had plagued my night, and couldn't do more than take what he fed me. Waiting to breathe at his whim, blurry gaze fixed to the nest of curls at his root. The dark trail that led up to his bellybutton.

"So fucking tight," he snarled, pressing in as deep as he could—stretching my pussy and my jaws at the same time. "Like I haven't already had you stuffed and stretched, gaping for me. Like you've never been touched and this pretty little pussy wasn't milking my balls dry, just yesterday."

It was then, as he held me immobile, stuffing me end to end, that he pulled his fingers free once more.

And traced the rim of my ass.

I bucked. Choking on cock, the veil of elite energy lifted for a brief instant of blinding panic as he tested that tight, puckered ring.

Chuckling, he let me take a tiny sip of air before forcing me back down. Deeper this time. Distracting me with one threat, while invading me with another. His finger breached my ass, lubricated by my own shame, the press burned. Slipping through until he reached the second knuckle and had to fight against my efforts to keep him out.

"Are you ready?" he asked, conversational with one finger burrowing through my bowels in tiny, taboo increments. Fucking my mouth with a sedate pace that left me reeling and without tether. "Are you going to beg for me to come down your throat? Beg to come with my finger in your ass as you swallow every, precious drop? Or"—he pulled his finger back, only to deepen the burn in a single, punishing thrust —"are you happy playing the martyr? Hiding behind your little shield, hating yourself for how much you want this?"

Head swimming in lust and fog, I couldn't speak when he pulled me free of his cock. Left his tip at my lips, inky black eyes boring deep into my soul. Where he held me in thrall and awaited his answer. Fingering my ass in a mockery of what I really wanted. What I needed, but couldn't voice.

Instead, panting, I reached for his balls. Pruney fingers finding that sack taut with unspent seed, I added a gentle, downward pressure just as he'd done in the shower.

Surprise flicked through those ebon depths, and he hissed, cock lurching where it sat poised to reclaim my mouth.

And then, in a rush of frigid air, the door swung open at my back. All that was obscene—dripping and stretched by my enemy—on full, sordid display.

"Well, *well*," came the amused drone of another man. The very *last* man I wanted to see as I choked on the captain's cock. As I braced on all fours, a finger buried in my ass, a cock all but ready to burst where it throbbed against my lips. "What have we here?"

14

I squealed, reacting only half as fast as the captain.

Abandoning my ass, wrenching my lips off his swollen prick, he shoved me into the deeper part of the bathing pool for an instant before I was drawn back and spun. My ribs clamped tight between his thighs, his cock twitching against my spine, he slipped one arm around my shoulders and covered my nipples with his forearm.

Submerged to my collarbones, I couldn't so much as blink when his influence seized me in a painful fist. The gold pumping through my veins forced me to sit utterly still. Rigid. Arousal frozen in my veins, despite the horror of seeing just who'd invaded this moment.

General Tilcot.

Murky brown eyes penetrating the surface of the

bathing pool, the general inspected every exposed inch of me he might claim. Already naked, but for the fluffy white towel slung loose about his hips, he grinned and said, "Asher, my boy, sorry to interrupt!"

Amplified in the small, wet room, the general's voice vibrated inside my chest and I flinched. Pressing deeper into the captain's embrace.

"Then leave," the captain snapped, absent any hint of respect for his superior.

"Come now," the general cooed, dropping his towel and splashing into the warm water before I could do more than glance away. "Don't be like that, boy. We're family."

The captain laughed, though it was an acidic, humorless sound. "Only when it suits you."

"I hope you're not still bitter about the paid leave and all the many, *many* allowances I've made for your safety, despite your flagrant disregard of protocol?" the general returned, condescension a thick ooze that spilled from his lips. And when he got no response, he issued a deep, theatrical sigh. Scooping up water in his big hands, he splashed it over his face and scrubbed at a very slight shadow of facial hair. "You must understand this was done for your own good. I'm trying to protect you and the girl."

Fingers tight enough to bruise, the captain hauled me closer. Enough that I could feel the tension humming through his thighs, where I was bracketed between them. "I think I can do without your brand of protection, Harper."

A wicked gleam illuminated those murky depths, and the general smirked. "And if you'd killed our wildcat on the battlefield? *Before* her power could be understood or utilized? What then?"

"If you'll recall," the captain said, his cultured drawl forced through tight lips and clenched teeth, "I was following *your* orders. You wanted her tested on the field before she'd even been assessed. Before Sasha even had a chance to evaluate her power and assess the risks."

"Well, now who's to say?" The general grinned. "I suppose, it really comes down to the word of a decorated general, or that of a captain of the special forces who's been taken off duty while he tries to get a handle on the priestess he claimed *without permission*. A girl labelled *'dangerous'* by the leader of her kind. And you should know, cousin," he added in a light, carefree tone, "there's a case to be made that she be removed from your care entirely. The capitol is considering the merits of giving her to someone more... *experienced* in the care of exceptional priestesses. After all, training an empath has never been done before, and given the potential the girl has shown, it would seem a risky endeavor to allow her management to be mishandled by an inexperienced soldier of insignificant rank."

Sensing the trap for what it was, the captain said nothing.

But I *felt* his reaction. What went unseen, still filtering through the shield with nothing to throttle it. Elite energy surged behind my ribs, a storm of possessive rage seething and spitting as the captain watched the other without blinking.

Utterly still, but for the thrashing of his heart and mine.

"You think I don't remember what it's like to take a priestess for the first time?" the general asked, spreading his arms along the rim of the pool to display an impressive wingspan and slabs of heavy, rippling muscle. "To be drunk on that sort of power?" He chuckled, inspecting me through a slimy grin. Seeming to take no notice of the tempest building at my back. "There's no parallel for such a gift, to say nothing of their tight little Tritan cunts."

The captain went rigid. His muscles going stiff where he held me locked in place. Arms a tight, protective band capable of leaving bruises marking me as his.

His to corrupt.

To control and stain.

"She's a drug, boy." Poised, cocky and confident, the general shrugged. "One that's clouded your judgement with the sweet taste of pussy and power. But they're all the same. Whores who need a firm hand and a fat cock." He glanced down, into the water where he grew thick with the promise of a brewing fight. "It'll take more than one to break her spirit. To kill the part of her that dreams of rebellion so you can fill the empty space with the behavior of your choice. She should be given no rest until she's well and truly broken in. Not so snug anymore, perhaps, but"—he made a face—"flawless obedience has its price. Besides, it won't be long before there's a new generation up for sale."

"Fuck off, Harper," the captain snarled, and surging upright, he brought me with him before I might react to that sentiment. Instead I hung stiff from his arms, gold pumping through my veins in a show of the captain's influence. His desperate need for control that bled into me. "I don't need you to tell me how to train my slave."

"If that were true," the general cooed, "wouldn't she be trained already?"

To this, the captain had nothing to say. Merely marched me toward the exit in a shower of sloshing water and naked flesh.

Straight into the general's path, though it couldn't be helped.

A rough palm landed on my navel. Fingertips splayed from hip to hip, the general's touch sent a screech to flounder and die in my throat. Caught and murdered before it was ever given life.

"I could make it an order..." General Tilcot murmured, and murky dark eyes slid up. Over my nudity, bypassing my face, to find the captain's furious glare where it simmered over my shoulder. "I could command you to leave her here, with me, and no one would question it. Some might even wonder why I've yet to take over. And who knows," he continued, fingers curling in to scrape at my reddened flesh with blunt nails. A threat that *almost* brushed the top of my hairless mound. "Perhaps she *is* different. Enough that she'd be of more use in the program as a bree—"

"We're done here," the captain snarled, and all but hurled me from the pool. Following me out to the sound of boisterous, cruel laughter.

"Of course you are, boy." Turning, the general folded his forearms and set his chin atop corded muscle. Coy, as he floated and watched. "This has been your pattern since you were a child. Always have to have the last word."

"See, now that's where you're wrong." Running a towel over my skin, the captain was rough. Hands shaking, he completely ignored my feminine charms in his haste to be gone, dragging rumpled pants over wet skin. "I'm leaving before you make a challenge I can't ignore. And," he tossed his shirt over his shoulder and turned to face the other elite, "I don't want your unborn child to grow up fatherless."

And with that, the captain threw open the door—the last word claimed as his.

It was my mistake to turn and look.

To make eye contact with the Caledonian general lounging in a pool of steaming water. Chin set atop crossed forearms, all shoulders, tousled hair, and tranquil muscle, he lifted the fingers of his left hand. Smirked, and gave me a dainty little wriggle that sent chills scampering down my spine.

15

All but naked, I staggered along at the captain's back. Dazed. Dragged along in his wake, I clutched a fluffy white towel over my breasts. Unable to shake the general's smirk, his absurd confidence in watching us go an ominous threat I could feel nipping at my heels.

Mind reeling at the hinted revelations—the half-truths and things I wasn't supposed to hear, much less understand—I did my best to keep pace with the captain's long-legged stride. Bare feet slapping at cool tiles, my jaw stretched with dull pain that spoke of the things I'd done. Opening for the captain with little more than gentle prompting.

I *ached*. Pussy throbbing with yet another release built and destroyed, blood still singing with elite might and denial.

Tangled in all things Asher, his fury became

mine. His need to flee living in my chest almost as surely as the taut misery between my legs pulsed heavy and low in his sack.

But something stood out above all else.

Above the fact that they were seemingly related, the threat of being claimed by the general, the constant lurking threat of the capitol's interest, and the consequences of what I had just allowed to happen.

"What program do you need Tritans for?" I asked, throat parched, dry and gritty as I watched the captain's shoulders tighten.

He said nothing.

"Asher—"

Spinning, he glowered down at me for the space of a single heartbeat, then took me by the shoulders and shoved me into a storage closet. "Enough," he snarled when the door snapped shut, plunging us into darkness. Bare chest heaving where it was pressed against mine, he shook me. Energy laced with a desperate, frantic edge. "Have you no concept of the danger we are in? Did you hear *nothing* that was just said?"

"Nothing I haven't already been threatened with," I returned, and stood my ground. Blood thick with the might of an elite, with a false bravado that left me flush with a confidence to which I had no rights.

"Then you weren't listening," he hissed, one hand finding my nape while the other landed high at the base of my throat. Forefinger and thumb pinching either side of my jaw, he tipped my head back. "He means to take you from me. To break you over a dozen cocks and see if you're the exception to the rule."

Sweat beaded at my brow, nausea bubbling in my throat, but I swallowed it back, and said, "What rule?"

At this, he grinned—and I saw it for the cruel, hateful thing it was, even through the dark. "Not your concern, little girl."

I laughed, high and brittle. "Not my concern? Asher! It's *my* life."

Fist wrenched free of my hair, he punched the wall beside my temple. Fingers squeezing where they were locked tight on my jaw, he bumped my skull into the wall and bellowed, "*And you're my slave!*" Forgetting to be covert, his voice filled the tiny closet to over flowing. Breath hot with scarcely restrained fury. "You have no rights! I could kill you here and now and no one would question it."

Skin flushed with his temper, I sneered. Reckless. "I shouldn't be surprised to learn you're related to that monster. You sound just like him. Same threats. One cock or a dozen, what's the difference?"

In an instant, the captain went still. Cold.

And then he swallowed.

Nodded.

Nostrils pinched white, he released me in a rush and stepped back. "Fine."

Without another word, he kicked the door open and burst into the hall. Dragging me along in his wake, we descended the stairs, passed by the crowd gathering at the doors of the harem, and burst into the morning sun where the cobbles were cold on my bare feet. Where the eyes of dozens of Caledonian soldiers flicked over my nearly nude frame with open interest.

We were stopped by a trio of armed soldiers.

Three elites, though they were unbound. Absent the energy boost enslaving a priestess afforded so many of their brethren.

"Rawlings," the largest said, chin dipping in a slight nod.

"Reese." Stepping in front of me, the captain blocked me front sight. "What brings you to this fine establishment in the middle of your shift?"

Flanking us, one of the others said, "We've orders to take your priestess directly to Sasha for training."

"Orders?" the captain drawled, head tilting toward the speaker. "From whom?"

"General Tilcot, sir," said a young man with the smoothest cheeks I'd ever seen. His uniform pristine, not a stitch out of place. "And I'm to escort you to the barracks for assessment, sir."

For a moment, I thought the captain would react beyond the thunderous scowl he sent back toward the second floor of the bathhouse. Dark flames lashed at the air between us, where his hands were hot and tight on my flesh. Reeking of possessive furor, until the captain issued a tight nod and turned to face me.

"Very well," he drawled, and affecting an air of nonchalance, he made a concentrated effort to withdraw from me. To take his energy and leave me swaying in the cold.

Alone.

Naked.

Staggered without him lurking in the darkest parts of my soul, he took everything. Left me with just enough strength to remain upright, and had the audacity to run calloused fingers through my hair, murmuring, "Can't leave Sasha with anything to work with, hmm? Causing all sorts of nasty little problems that might get you killed. Trust me, pet," he said, a perfect mimic of mocking tone the general had used only minutes before. "It's for your own good. I'm trying to protect you from horrors you cannot even begin to imagine. We share the same blood, after all, General Tilcot and I. Just can't seem to help myself."

Robbed of my vitality, I swooned beneath his hands. Too weak to voice the vitriol, I was left starving for just a sip of the power he'd fed me just to show he could.

But with the void, came the shock of clarity.

In his absence, the veil began to fade.

I could see. What he'd been doing. How easily

he'd slipped beneath my skin and left corruption in his wake.

He'd manipulated me.

Easily.

"Don't fret, Rawlings," Reese said, flashing the captain a quick, greasy smirk. "Aiden and I will get her there, all snug an' in perfect health."

The captain hummed, tugged his damp shirt off his shoulder, and slipped it over my head. Buttons already fastened, he reached beneath the damp material and worked my arms through the sleeves. Inky gaze avoiding my eyes, he said, "Orders are orders," under his breath, then rolled the excess fabric until the cuffs of his dress shirt were cinched around my elbows.

"Captain Rawlings, sir," the smooth-cheeked elite stammered. "You can't wear... *that* to a meeting with the general!"

Lifting his shoulder, the captain said, "Then hand over your shirt, Collins, and let's be on our way."

The boy's face flushed a blistering shade of red, and with trembling fingers, he reached for his collar to do just that.

"Oh, for shit sakes!" Reese snapped, giving the younger man a shove. "Stop by the captain's residence on your way to HQ." The burly elite stepped up to my back, slipping one hand around my elbow. "Priestess."

I swallowed, fighting the urge to shuck his touch,

to look to the captain for guidance—to beg forgiveness if it meant I might be saved from the ravenous hunger whipping at the back of my skull before something came of it. Trying not to let the shock of revelation show on my face before I'd had the time to sort through my thoughts.

Instead, I ground my molars. Fists clenched at my sides, I clung to what little remained of my pride.

And said nothing.

Sasha would have the answers. She could wade through the confusion of foggy lust lingering between my temples.

She could fix the shield and give me the power I needed to be free. Only she could give me distance from a man who could take at will, wielding the might of a priestess *and* an elite without a hint of strain or effort.

For if not her, who?

The Head Priestess of Tritan faith, a woman made of secrets and dressed in power, who could teach me to counter the captain's attacks without succumbing to the infection of elite energy and the fury squirming in my heart.

A beast named empath.

It had been left to starve, awakened by the captain's petty cruelty.

Without a backward glance, I turned to follow these new elites.

Dazed.

Ravenous.

Dressed in nothing but the captain's shirt and a wet towel, I shivered with the weight of inky, black eyes tracking me through the thinning crowd, but refused him the satisfaction of seeing my confusion.

Every step bought distance.

Each breath I took a cleansing of my soul, despite the masculine scent clinging to my shirt or the slick glide lingering between my thighs.

None of it was mine.

Manufactured to manipulate, an artful lie I hadn't seen before it was too late.

It wasn't long before the Tilcot manse came into view. Before I was once again padding through the illustrious halls of white marble lined with stolen art. This time absent a guide, we headed toward Sasha's office in silence.

And when I saw the Head Priestess's drab, unassuming door swing into view I stifled the urge to bolt. To throw priceless Eloran art to the floor and sprint to my destination for no other reason than I hadn't the strength.

Instead, I waited for Reese to open the door. Ushering me inside with a nod to the woman inside, he closed the door with a gentle snap.

"Mila," she said, voice a soft croon that drew a rush of heated shame to wet my lashes. "Welcome."

I wasted nothing for subtlety, forcing, "Help me,"

through the points of my canines. "Sasha, *please*. My shield. It didn't work. He found it and—"

Standing in a rush, she rounded the corner and cupped my cheeks in palms that were soft and warm. "Take a breath. That's it. Nice and deep." Brushing heated skin in a sweep of her thumbs, she wiped away the salty wetness so I might see the deep, furrowed lines bunched between her brows. "Have a seat."

I sat. Unfurling the cuffs of my borrowed shirt, I twisted the gloomy fabric between my fingers. Drawn in by her touch. The soothing promise in soft skin. My mouth watered at the precious hint of priestess energy oozing through her palms, where she cupped my cheeks and probed me with a tiny spike of soothing purity.

"Tell me, child."

"It didn't even slow him down," I rasped, squeezing my eyes shut as if that alone could turn the tide on my hunger. "But the captain sends his compliments. Called your shield ingenious, or something to that effect."

She frowned, for her energy lanced through the barren waste the captain had left in his wake, and found nothing she might work with. Nothing with which she could use to soothe me—I felt it happen.

Saw the way the wrinkle between her brows deepened, and knew the scent of fear for the tantalizing whisper it was.

"Help me," I whispered again.

She stepped back. Face arranged in a careful mask of concern, she bumped a hip against her desk. "Captain Rawlings managed all that, did he?"

I nodded, tone an echoing void of empty destruction when I said, "Before breakfast."

Ignoring the risk, she took my hands and put a stop to the anxious twisting. And I felt her try again, to pull from an empty cup. "Everything will be okay."

"Don't you see?" I laughed, and launched myself from the chair. Evicted from her presence before I succumbed to the temptation. Before I turned the tide and sent an inferno ripping through her palms, so I might feed from a well of a once-powerful priestess. "*Nothing* is okay, Sasha! He left me with nothing, can't you feel it?"

"Mila, please. I need you to sit and relax so we can begin to sort this out. We'll try something different, this time. I have to admit I didn't expect"—she pushed a hand through her silver-blonde hair and glanced to the door—"didn't think the captain had come quite so far in his explorations. But we expected this. That things would be different for you." A breath whistled through her nose. "There's a way we can dampen your empathic abilities. We just have to find what works."

A wash of cold awareness settled over me.

Twisting and sick, it stuck to my nape and oozed from the back of my skull, forward.

Realization.

The Head Priestess' icy blue eyes flicked back to the door.

This was just another betrayal.

She didn't want to help me tame the empath.

She wanted to destroy it.

The only weapon our enslaved people might possess, the only scrap of power that didn't lie between thighs forced to spread or knees purpled with bruises.

I should have expected nothing less.

"You were right," I breathed, and felt a stillness bleed through my chest. "Right and so very, *very* wrong." It was my turn to touch, and I did it without thought. Claimed her hands in fingers that had become deadly, hooked claws. "I am nothing but a plaything. No talent. No skill. Defenseless against a man like Captain Asher Rawlings." I took a step. Forced her back. "There's nothing but hunger. A thirst for more. And he made me like it, Sasha. Just like he promised he could."

Sasha's pale skin went a sickly shade of green. "He ignored my warning. That stupid boy!"

I cracked my neck, pointed teeth flashing at the question that wasn't. "He served me a diet rich in elite energy and Infected me with the need to be fucked raw by a man I hate. An enemy. A man I want to see brought to his knees before me." A choked sob splintered over my lips, but I couldn't stop the admission from spilling over. "And I *liked* the taste. If he were here now," I whispered, and felt the salty burn of tears when they spilled over my lashes, "I would go to my knees, right here. Right in front of you. I'd choke him down and beg for more. Just another... little... taste..."

"You have to fight this, Mila," she said, standing tall before me. Broken, but unbent. "Fight the empath, and it will pass."

"Yes," I hissed, and didn't blink. "That's what you want for me, isn't it? To learn to bend before I break? To learn to love the bruises on my knees, as you do."

She swallowed and it was dry. I heard the click of her throat working.

Thumbs working back, I traced the fine bones in her wrists. "Because I can't beat him, can I? Not as I am. So why bother fighting at all?"

"This isn't you, Mila." Icy blue eyes flicked to the door. "It's the empath."

"But that's not *entirely* true, is it?" I drawled, licking dry lips. "He showed me, Sasha. What you wouldn't. That priestesses and elites are two sides of the same coin." Jaw flexing, my head tilted to the side and I watched her every tiny movement. "And then he showed me what could be done with it."

Again, her eyes flicked to the door. "It doesn't work like that, Mila. Once we are bound, there's nothing we can do to stop them using our power."

I sneered. "Ah, yes. It keeps coming back to the

chains, doesn't it?" I glanced at the covered pedestal on the far side of her office, where an unused set sat hidden beneath dark cloth. "A convenient shield for *you* to hide behind, hmm? One that absolves you of your sins in this war."

Cold blue sparks leapt at me. "You think you can judge me, child?" she whispered, deadly soft. And then, turning her wrists and setting her grip to my forearms, she abandoned all pretense at soothing the beast. Provoked to show her temper for what it really was. "You've been a slave for days. This has been my life for five years."

"What program do they need Tritans for?" I asked. Soft, so she'd have to strain to hear me. So I could watch when her cheeks went sallow and her pupils dilated.

Her lips parted, but nothing came out.

Then, once more, she glanced at the door—and I knew. Who she was waiting for, who was coming to check on his priestess after working so hard to separate me from the captain's delicate sphere of protection.

An admission of guilt I could see and feel.

Despite the familiar pain of betrayal, a grin spread over my lips. "I should have wondered," I said, "when you called me a plaything for an elite. Should have wondered how you knew." A froth of seething wrath bubbled up, reaching for the pretty pure energy swirling before me, meager though it was.

"That I'm just another tool—a hole to be used and filled. *Soiled*. Pretty words from like recognizing like."

Cheeks beating hot, she reeled back and slapped me full across the face. "*Mila*! Pull yourself together," she snarled, fending off the barbs of wicked hunger probing through her modest defenses. "You're going to get yourself killed."

I paid the sting less attention than the warning. "What you don't see, Sasha, what you don't understand?" I hummed, and tongued a bit of coppery warmth spilling over my lip. "I don't have to bend. I don't have to break. All I have to do is *become*."

At my back, the door opened without the courtesy of a knock.

16

General Harper Tilcot.

Broad shoulders filling the entire doorway, he blocked the light. The exit. Any and all hope of an escape that didn't go through him, first.

Despite the chaotic blizzard thrashing behind my ribs, I let my eyes fall. Affecting the demure gaze of a slave—and felt Sasha's entire frame sag in relief.

But still, her grip did not loosen.

She was poised to counter any move I might make against her beloved master. To wrap the empath in chains before I could be unleashed, for what she really wanted wasn't to foster a rebellion using my unpredictable gifts.

She wanted obliteration of the empath.

For me to be submissive and compliant. To follow along in her perfect, dainty footsteps, never setting a hair out of line lest I disturb the careful balance she had achieved here.

Asher wanted to take. To control all that I was and use me for his own ends. A power source, an obedient sleeve for his cock, he wanted to *possess*.

But General Tilcot?

I blinked, watching the large man move from beneath a coy fan of my lashes.

He wanted a weapon.

"How goes the training of my wildcat?" he asked, slipping the door closed behind us with a firm snap. "I'm here for good news, Sasha."

The Head Priestess swallowed. "It's an... adjustment," she replied, careful with her words. Artful. "Training an empath is going to be a difficult journey, but I'm confident—"

Snapping his fingers, the general took an impatient step toward us. "What is she capable of? What are her limits? Her strengths?"

"I—" Sasha cleared her throat, fingers growing tight and slick around my wrist. "I haven't had the chance to fully assess her, sir."

A condescending sound bubbled up from deep inside the general's deep chest.

"I needed to make sure she was grounded, first. That she could handle the strain of being tested without irritating her empathetic nature."

Humming, the general said, "Ah, yes. An empath. Such a rare creature." He closed the distance between us in only two steps. "Tell me more. Everything that makes her an exception to the rule."

"I—I don't understand, sir," Sasha stammered, and tried to pull me back.

But I did.

At least in part.

It was a phrase I'd already heard—before the captain had ushered me to the safety of continued ignorance.

And it seemed the general was in the mood to share.

"This fragile, *dangerous* girl seems to be more powerful than half of my best priestesses combined," he began. "I'd like to know what other... hidden talents she might have. An eye for art, perhaps?" He grinned, plucking at the captain's baggy shirt where it had fallen to expose my shoulder. "A sense of the future before it occurs?"

Sasha exhaled a nervous chuckle. "No, sir. Not that I'm aware of—"

"Then perhaps she carries more than a barren desert in place of a womb, hmm?"

All the color rushed from the Head Priestess' face. Her fingers slick with cold sweat where they tightened then grew slack on my skin. "S-sir, that's not... I don't—"

"Is it possible," he pressed, and took the top button of my shirt in between long fingers. Working it free without so much as touching my skin, he took liberties without paying the price. "Might she be bred? An exception to the rule of infertile priestesses?"

She swallowed, *hard*—a sentiment that resonated. Deep, where revulsion sparked and grew, disgust and terror became something... more.

Glancing my way, Sasha paused before she said, "It... it's *possible*." It was an admission that saw the general nod then work another two buttons free to expose the modest swell of my cleavage. "But if any elite c-could get her with... with child," she said, stumbling over her words, "then it would be Captain Rawlings. Sir. As the only elite bound to an empath, their bond is unique. It has properties we haven't yet begun to unravel."

The general sighed. "Yes. I rather expected you to say as much. But what if," he mused, and abandoned the effort to undress me. Moving instead to the far side of the Head Priestess' desk, where a pedestal sat covered in dark cloth. "What if another claim were to supersede the first, hmm? A *stronger* claim from an elite already bound to a powerful priestess."

Sasha's jaw worked around nothing. Soundless rejection of a heinous idea she hadn't been expecting to refute. I felt the cascade of emotions sparkle through her touch, tempting me to reach out and take. To revel in that sweet revulsion and *drink*.

Lifting one bulky shoulder, the general shrugged. "It's worth a shot, no?"

And with that, he pulled the curtain back on the chains. Revealed the golden manacles that were a match to my own, and said, "Come here, girl."

I went. Willingly. Shooting Sasha a demur flick of my eyes before I pulled free of her restraining grip, I ignored the warning that sparkled through my skin. An alarm that was silenced the instant the contact between us broke. Pale legs flashing as I moved to obey, I moved on silent feet, eyes dutifully trained on the floor.

Where a good slave ought to look.

It was, after all, what they all wanted. Trained obedience that concealed the truth of pushing women to be desperate and coy in exchange for their own survival.

"General Tilcot, sir, I *really* don't think—"

"Then be silent," he said, cutting her off. "We've been over what your job is, Sasha. And women don't do their best thinking on their backs, do they?"

My lip curled where he couldn't see it.

But I held myself in tight control. Watching without blinking. Fixated on this elite who didn't see the danger standing directly before him, who chose to ignore the other half of the coin, and saw only the healer.

Ignoring the destroyer as he couldn't ignore the hidden promise of my nipples.

I fought the smile.

Watched as he withdrew the chains and lay them

out on the desktop to his left—one by one—then claimed my hand in one that was smooth and dry. Manicured. *Soft.*

Churning, lazy flames licked the back of my wrist. Power in dizzying abundance, yet it lacked the captain's flavor, the pure ambrosia of vitality I'd grown accustomed to in so short a time.

I took a careful sip.

Groaned before I could stop myself, and rolled my neck. Trying not to take more than a single gulp, I turned the tide before the empath slipped her leash, and said, "Tell me what the program is for."

The general snorted. Collecting one manacle, he slipped it over my knuckles and fit it over the one already welded in place. "Bossy little thing, hmm?"

Stretching unfamiliar muscles, I sent a single, tiny barb darting through the general's veins. Took that dainty sip I'd stolen, and put the energy to work. Clumsy and reckless, I got the sense of the man in careful, lapping waves.

"Tell me," I whispered, bleeding through muscle and sinew. Tugging on random strings until I felt a thread of compliance sparkle through his meaty brain.

Manipulating.

Infecting.

As Sasha had done to me. And Asher. Both more proficient in the art of wielding another's energy, both lacking the pure, unfiltered rage that sang in my blood.

"The program..." Murky brown eyes flicked up to meet mine, and the general frowned. "It's for Tritans. For the good of the... empire..." Elite energy surged to life. Laced with confusion, tainted with alarm, the general took a breath. "What is this?"

I couldn't help it—I grinned my toothiest grin.

And lost control of the empath in a second.

She surged to the fore. Skating through flesh, drawn to the buffet of banked flames peppered with a tantalizing whisper of fear, my palm landed on the general's broad chest.

Closing the loop.

Beneath my palm, the beat of a healthy heart.

Strong. Rhythmic and steady.

Until I found a soft spot and burrowed deep as I might go.

Drinking my fill. Gorging on the strength of a man who'd taken everything from my people. Whose very life force was laced with the beauty of priestess magic.

A large hand wrapped about my throat, but I paid it no mind. Lost in the seduction of indulging myself, I feasted. Replacing all that Asher had stolen. Reveling in the way that strong pulse broke down and grew erratic, I grew entranced by the sour sweat beading on the general's brow.

"You... little... *bitch*," he rasped, face blooming a

deep shade of ruddy purple. Sagging before me, he slumped in the chair. Chest heaving for breath, spittle misting the narrow space between us, the general's hand fell away as his eyes grew round. The whites speckled with tiny dots of blood-red.

"My turn."

I heard the words before their meaning registered. Before the eerie echo could take root and give warning of an attack.

Cool hands slipped over my collarbones, framing my shoulders and throat.

"Release him, *empath*," the Head Priestess spat, fitting me with a noose of blinding, white priestess magic. The sort of purity I was forbidden to wield.

And it was then, as I felt her energy slip through my wide-open defenses, that I realized my colossal error—in taking from the general, I'd given Sasha leverage. A window to shut, energy Asher had taken with the intent to leave her with nothing to work with.

Nothing that might get me killed.

"Let me do this," I hissed, caught in an easy thrall of a master. "I can beat him, Sasha. I can be the weapon we need."

"They'll execute you for this, *and I should let them.*"

"Sasha—"

She forced me back. Took a liberal helping of the general's energy and built a wall around the ravenous beast that couldn't be reasoned with. "You think to embody both sides of the spectrum?" She laughed, low and cruel. "To be the hero we need in this war? You're nothing more than a delusional little girl. A child playing with forces she cannot possibly understand."

With both hands, she sent me staggering back. Crashing into the desk before I hit the floor in a disoriented heap of bare legs and an oversized shirt. The towel fallen, tangled between my ankles.

"Go," she snapped. "Now, before they realize what you've done here."

I blinked, trying to banish the encroaching fog. "Sasha—"

"I said *go!*" Whirling, she turned back to the fallen general and set her hands to his face. The hands of a healer, working to revive a destroyer.

I stood on legs that trembled, staggering toward the door. Haunted by the image of the Head Priestess stooping over a man who'd taken so much from our people. From *her.*

"And Mila?" she said, not bothering to look up from her rotten work. "Pray."

17

Frost.

It tingled across the surface of my skin. Crystalized in each and every pore and left me cold, right through to my middle. Numb. Utterly so.

A blank void absent any meager scrap of energy—priestess or elite—I was untethered, left to watch as the world tilted and spun around me. Run off its axis by the weight of the Head Priestess' shackles. That gleaming wall of pure, unusable energy caging me inside myself.

Staggering, I crashed into the wall before I could find a door knob. Before I managed to slip from Sasha's office without daring to fully open the door. Keeping the carnage I'd wrought hidden away in the dark, where the Head Priestess scrambled to fix it despite my very best efforts.

"Ready to go, Wildcat?" Marco asked, and set one steadying hand on my shoulder. Sent, no doubt, by none other than Captain Asher Rawlings, for despite the way we'd parted, he was not the sort of man to give up possession of his favorite toy without a fight.

Reese and Aiden flanked the office without bothering to glance my way. No doubt waiting for the general to return and issue his orders.

I nodded at the captain's man, and my chin hit my chest before I managed to recover. "Let's go," I rasped, sweating and cold. Yet despite fleeing the scene of my crime, I did as I was told, and prayed...

... for the general to die, no matter how hard Sasha tried to save him.

We collected Gabe outside of the manse, but for me, the walk to the captain's residence passed in a blur of numb. A fog I couldn't squint hard enough to see through. I heard nothing of their banter, my head lost in the swirling mists of delirium—caught somewhere between blood lust and exhaustion. Victory and defeat, for I'd held the general's life in my hand, felt him squirm and thrash and flounder.

And I'd been ready to extinguish all that he was.

The payment had been my only ally.

Sasha revealed as another traitor with an agenda I couldn't see and wasn't invited to understand.

Teeth clenched, I shook my head to dispel the ache of regret.

It was, after all, a lesson I'd learned long ago. That

friends were nothing but a weakness, an opportunity for future betrayal.

I was an island no man could touch.

Alone.

Always.

Except for *Asher*.

"Not sure if the captain is back yet," Marco said, jerking me from my thoughts, "but it's probably best if you wait for him upstairs."

I blinked, a haze of blackness dotting the edges of my vision as I was escorted to the stairs. Compliant and docile, for no other reason than I hadn't the strength for war. Not with this new cage wrapped tight around what pitiful little remained of my power.

The empath in chains of blinding priestess magic.

Instead, I allowed the soldier to guide me. One hand on my back, his mundane energy not nearly significant enough to tempt the beast to so much as rattle the bars of her cage.

But when we reached the captain's door, I mustered a smile. My best approximation of a meek and well-behaved slave. "Thank you, Marco," I said, pleased when he took a startled step back, "for the escort."

Eyes darting to the captain's bedroom door, Marco blinked, but said nothing at all as I retreated. Making every effort to be silent, I placed my hand on the heavy oak and turned the knob.

The soft click of the lock sliding home was

masked by Marco's incredulous, "I think that's the first time she's spoken directly to me. *Gabe!*"

I slipped inside the captain's room on silent feet as Marco thundered down the stairs. Pressing my back to the solid door to gather my wits, I tried to clear my sight of the sparkle of dark stars narrowing my vision to a tight tunnel.

When I took my next breath, it was to find the captain sitting behind his desk in the dark. Head resting on steepled fingers. A decanter of rich amber liquid pinched between his elbows, his gaze was unfocused, but fixed to the contents. Watching it shimmer and swirl. On his brow, lines etched deep into the surface, tracing the crease at his eyes, hiding behind the raspy stubble shadowing his cheeks and jaw.

He looked tired.

Vulnerable.

My mouth watered, and I took a step.

"Mila," he said without looking up, unsurprised that I was standing in his space. A lurking, vengeful shade in desperate need. "You're back sooner than I thought."

I said nothing. Pushing off the door, I staggered toward the well of vibrant, hypnotic flames I knew were waiting to soothe this pain. This bottomless ache of hunger denied time and again.

One *he* had caused.

One only he could free me from.

At my silence, he turned to look. Inky gaze falling to where his shirt sagged across my breastbone. My cleavage all but spilling free, the towel long since having fallen away.

His lips parted, pupils dilating with a slow pulse as his jaw grew tight at the corners—but the words died on his tongue. The concern turning to smoldering jealousy that peppered the air between us with tension.

With the bitter scent of anger.

Tongue darting out, I wet my lips and prepared to bend like the desperate, coy whore they'd wanted me to become. Padding across the floor until I was close enough to reach, until my fingertips brushed the hard pectorals I knew were secreted away beneath a fresh, crisp shirt.

I reached for it.

Took what I wanted…

… because for this, I needed no permission.

He sucked a breath between his teeth. Turning to face me, his lap was made available.

Without shame or hesitation, I climbed into his chair. Knees spread beneath the tails of a borrowed shirt, I hooked my calves through the arms of the chair and claimed my perch.

"Asher, *please*," I whispered, and spread my palms across the ridges of his collarbones. "It hurts…"

The captain swallowed, watching me through twin pricks of obsidian that glittered in the half light.

But the clink of metal on metal intruded on this moment. Ensnared his attention and tore it away from my efforts to beg for what I needed. To play the whore and seduce.

He captured my wrist and found a spare manacle jangling where the general had left it. The attempt to claim me obvious, for the chains had no other purpose. "Harper," he spat, and pulled the golden bracelet over my knuckles and tossed it onto his desk. "Did he—"

"Please," I said again. "It hurts." I took his hand and place that rough, calloused palm on my breastbone.

Where I'd been left bare.

Touched by another man.

Exposed.

Encouraging his fingers to spread so he might feel what the Head Priestess had done to me, I bade him look deep inside, where only he might see the hurt and undo it as he had before.

"I'll give it to you," I breathed, and shivered when his free hand found purchase on my hip. Grip hesitant, but firm. "The empath. You can have it if you make the pain stop..."

A breath puffed over his lips. Pupils blown wide enough that they swallowed any subtle hint of color there might have been in his dark gaze.

"Help me." Hips tilting, I ground against him, knowing just what this game required of me. That the naked, melting flesh between my legs was a lure he could not resist when it traced the growing bulge at his inseam. "Please," I gasped. "Look what she did to me."

Sending a barb of pure, electric heat singing through my chest, he looked and saw the wall the Head Priestess had built.

"I can't feel *anything*," I whispered. "She took it all. Asher"—I swallowed, breath hitching when his fingers tightened at the sound of his name on my lips—"I'm so hungry... *so cold...*"

Shuddering beneath me, the captain relented. Worked to unravel all that Sasha had done, he sent fire to cleanse me of her influence. Chipping away at the shackles that held me in thrall, he thawed me of the frosted ice.

A tiny, fractured moan bubbled up and I sagged against him. Forehead dipping as the sparkling haze began to fade. As he warmed me, bit by bit.

"Do it, then," he whispered, hips flexing against the spot where I was wet and aching and warm. "Take what you need, little empath. My warrior priestess."

I couldn't help myself—I groaned. Set loose, free to indulge, I slipped beneath his skin and drank.

Just as I had with the general.

Just as Asher had taught me.

I gave the empath all she might ever want and settled back to watch the carnage unfold.

With scarcely more than an errant thought, the

heart thudding between us grew erratic. His touch between my breasts growing sweaty before the blunt scrape of nails scored my skin.

"What..." He gasped. Seized my wrist, and brought my manacles to life. Freezing me where I straddled him, the pulse of molten gold surged through my veins.

But it was too late.

I was already inside.

Already drinking from a cup named vengeance, I was messy and wild. Free to indulge the joy of claiming this power over an elite.

The elite.

The one who'd paid a mere fifty dollars for my freedom.

Who'd bound me for eternity with joy singing in his shriveled black heart.

The very man who'd taken my innocence from the back with rough hands and rougher words that had left marks too deep to wash away. Marks that couldn't be cleansed with mere fire, and couldn't be withered by a deep frost.

He'd promised to make me like it. To use pleasure to punish. To make me beg and swallow down every... single... drop...

And I had promised not to stop until every one of his kind lay dead at my feet.

No matter the cost.

That I might die trying.

I crooned as I felt his heart stutter and spit. Grinned when he bared blunt teeth and hissed without managing to utter a single word. And when his hand fell away, his influence flickering to a dull hum, I moved to take the rest of it.

To take *everything* he had left.

Because I didn't need permission.

Not for this.

Agony lanced through my chest, shot down my left arm, and floundered behind my ribs—but still, I pressed on. Gulping him down despite the sweat beading on my brow. Ignoring the way the room spun and a peculiar, familiar tingle prickled at my lips.

And so I didn't noticed when my vision tunneled down to a narrow point once more.

Not until I slumped against him.

Boneless.

All but unable to force a breath through the ring of frost gripping my lungs in a frigid grip, my cheek pressed to his shoulder.

"*Sssstop*," he hissed, but that was all.

Nothing else could penetrate the ravenous dark when it yawned around us...

... and swallowed us whole...

18

A deep, rumbling groan echoed in my ears. Dragging me back from the edge of the void into a land of slicing agony. Where my every muscle ached with exertion and the petting, rough hands that sought to soothe left only misery in their wake.

"Mmph," I grunted, incoherent and flailing. Knowing just who would take such liberties, I tried to push him away from me. *"Don't."*

A slap landed on my cheek. Gentle yet jarring, a command for me to, "Wake up."

I groaned as warm breath caressed my cheeks. "Get off," I mumbled, mouth full of starch. Powdery and dry beyond anything I'd ever known. My tongue tacked to the roof of my mouth with a thick, gluey paste.

"Mila. *Wake* up," he hissed. "What did you do? The fuck was that?" he asked, and everything shifted. Skin raking over a carpet, I was dragged into his lap. Head lolling on a flimsy, boneless neck before he thought to support me. Before he pushed the hair back from my damp forehead and went still. Cradling me in arms that trembled with the effort.

"Kept my promise," I whispered without bothering to peel my lids apart. And then, after a moment's thought, "*Failed* to keep my promise."

I felt him frown, felt his displeasure crackle against skin made hypersensitive by the flood of too much energy, too fast. Energy that had been wasted. "What are you on about? *What did you do?*"

Laughter bubbled up, surprising us both, when I said, "Well... to start, I tried to kill you, Asher."

For a moment, he was silent. Fingers running tiny, infuriating circles against my nape, he seemed to consider my words. And then, "You..."

"Tried to kill you, yes." Squinting, I managed to crack my left eye so I might see what I could feel so clearly. The shock, the subtle glimmer of anger, but best of all, the begrudging admiration. The intrigue and the arousal. "Almost got the general, too," I added, wrinkling my nose, "but Sasha stopped me. The sneaky traitor."

Going stiff, the captain's already waxy face blanched a sickly shade of green. "You made an attempt on the general's life? General *Tilcot*?"

But to this, I had nothing to say. Merely waited for him to draw his own conclusions.

"Shit," he hissed, and his grip tightened. "*Shit!*" Head tilted back to bump against his desk, he laughed, low and rich. An incredulous bark of mirth that brought a helpless smirk to my own lips. "Do you have any idea what you've done?" he asked, and I watched his throat work around an anxious swallow. "All my plans, undone in a single shitty afternoon. Six grueling months in the West, all for nothing."

Stretching, I turned my nose into the crook of his elbow—where his sleeve was rolled up and his skin was bare—allowing myself to luxuriate in the flavor of panic. In the scent of the man I couldn't escape. "No promotion for you, hmm?"

Twice more, he thumped his skull against the desk. "He's going to kill you for this. You know that, right?" And then, dumping me onto the floor in a rubbery heap, he said, "Fuck*sakes*, I'm going to be sick."

Unable to move, I watched him crawl. Watched when he caught the rim of a garbage can with the tips of trembling fingers and pulled it as close as he could before retching. Sides heaving with a violent purge.

"Ughhh," he groaned and spat into the bucket. "The fuck did you do to me?"

"You're the healer," I drawled, feeling nausea bubble at the back of my own throat. "You figure it out."

He turned his head enough to scowl at me—and vomited again. "Why?" he asked, sweating and pale. Almost grey beneath the bronze-tinged skin. "Why would you attack Tilcot? Of all the fucking—"

"And why not?" I returned. "He's a monster. You know it better than I do, captain." I snorted. "Why would I pass up the opportunity to remove the head of the snake?"

"You stupid little girl!" he hissed, and hunched over his bucket. "Harper isn't the head of anything. The empire has dozens more lined up to take his place." He paused to spit into the pail. "Dozens more who will be promoted to fill that void. The *only* thing his death means is a reshuffling of the ranks." Sagging back, he resumed his position, propped up against the desk. A pukey bucket pinched between spread knees. "All you've done is thrown fuel on a fire and draw attention of much worse men than Harper Tilcot."

Struggling, I managed to force myself upright. Claimed the spot next to him, and asked, "Is there a better way to kill elites?"

He rolled his eyes and swiped at his forehead with the back of his arm, blotting his brow. "Just can't help yourself, can you? I should chain you up and lock you in the cellar." Turning, he eyed the bottle of amber liquor perched on the edge of his desk. Grunted, and with a truly impressive effort, managed to throw his right arm up and knock the decanter to the floor.

It landed with a heavy thud, intact.

And with quaking fingers, he twisted the cap and sloshed alcohol all over himself. Soiling his now sweat-soaked shirt with the reek of spirits.

When he managed to get the rim to his lips, he took a swig, rinsed his mouth, then spat into the bucket with a grimace. A wrinkled nose. "But it's too late now, isn't it?" he murmured, again bringing the decanter to his lips. This time, drinking deep. His throat bobbing around each greedy swallow. "I don't know if I can fix this."

"I don't need your help."

Peering at me through a bleary, obsidian glare, he settled back and set his forearms to the bend in his knees. Bottle dangling from hooked fingers, a tiny, sinister smirk curled at the edge of his lips. "Ahh, yes. Such a fascinating delusion."

It was my turn to scowl. "What?"

"You called me a parasite, once," he murmured. "Insinuated elites are nothing without a priestess to kneel for them."

"That's not—"

"Remind me," he drawled, took another swig, then set the noxious garbage pail aside. "Who did you come to? Who did you beg to ease your pain?"

Throat thick, I shook my head on a denial I couldn't voice.

"You begged for it, Mila. Knelt over my cock, absent even the barest whisper of a fight. Dripping for it..." He smiled, and it sent terror spilling down my spine. "Making all *sorts* of offers and promises if only I could help you..."

Too weak to retreat, I could only sit there and wait. Knowing what came next. That this would be his greatest pleasure, despite everything that had come before.

And with shaking fingers, he reached and claimed the spot at my nape. Pulled me in tight so I might hear it when he whispered, "You're mine now, little empath. Body and soul. Gave yourself to me. *Willingly.*" Fingers carding through my hair, back to front, he let his thumb wander. Tracing my cheekbone down to my lips. "As easy as flipping a coin."

I exhaled the bitter flavor of defeat, eyes drifting closed on the pain of such a blow.

It was obvious, now. In the desolate vacuum of my defeat.

I wasn't the avenging hero, the liberator, or the righteous weapon Tritan needed for salvation.

I was exactly as they'd named me.

A delusional little fool, a child playing with forces I had no real understanding of.

And it was in that moment, as the captain closed the loop and claimed the empath for himself, I knew.

There was but a single living soul who embodied both sides of the spectrum—and he was *elite.*

Captain Asher Rawlings.

Enemy.

Conquering villain.

A master of this game to which I was hopelessly unequal.

When I held my silence, I felt him nod. "Here," he murmured. "You look like you need this."

The decanter hovered before my face. Amber liquid sloshing with a hollow tinkle that drew a reflexive swallow to my throat. Urging me to indulge.

I took the offering only for it to slip from clammy, weak fingers.

Without a word, the captain reclaimed the bottle and set it to my lips. Guiding my head back. Feeding me a burning sip, he filled my mouth until I could hold no more and the corners of my lips spilled over.

"Swallow," he murmured, wiping at the spillage with the pad of his thumb.

I obeyed.

Spluttered then coughed when it was down, pressing the back of one trembling hand to my lips.

"So." He took another long draught, throat working mechanically as he watched me. "You tried to kill me."

For a moment, as the spirits warmed my belly, I simply held his ebon gaze. Too tired to fight, too battered for anything resembling defiance. And then my chin dipped in a single, tight nod.

"I'll admit," he drawled, and the corner of his lips

twitched, "I'm impressed. But what concerns me is how spectacularly you failed."

Jaw tight, I scowled and looked away.

"I can feel it, you know." Setting the bottle between us, he grimaced and pushed himself to stand. "The damage you did to my heart reflected back into yours." Swaying, he clutched at the desk for a moment before adding, "Clever. Reckless and *incredibly* stupid, but a valiant attempt."

I snorted, watching him hobble to the bathroom with garbage pail in hand. "Thanks."

"It means we're linked, Mila," he said. "More deeply than I thought possible. It would seem, what is dangerous for one, is deadly to the other."

You cannot kill him without also killing yourself...

Realization flooded through my veins. Sluggish and befuddled, but stark in the knowledge that I'd heard this warning before—from the lips of the Head Priestess herself.

Asher's death would mean my own.

"Of course it does," I murmured when he closed the door. Letting the water run where I couldn't see.

And without much intention, I dragged myself upright. Fighting to remain standing, I clung to the edge of his desk and swayed. Dizzy. Sweating and cold. Breasts all but spilling free where my borrowed shirt sagged open, my heart strained to work. Pulse throbbing wildly beneath my jaw.

The glimmer of gold caught my attention, and I hooked the manacle with my forefinger, pulling it toward me in a bid to distract from the way my pulse thrashed beneath my jaw. A piece of an unused set.

Tritan chains.

It was a simple circlet of gold. Nothing remarkable, except for the way it glittered in the gloom. Except for what it meant for the women left scared in the empire's never-ending fight for dominance.

Because it always came back to the chains, didn't it? They couldn't control us without them, couldn't fight each other without first climbing through the ranks of the powerful and privileged.

I didn't react when the captain returned, breath heavy with the scent of mint.

Didn't flinch when he said, "He's wanted a second priestess since the moment he claimed his first." And with a ginger touch, he took the golden manacle with a frown and caught my eye. "He made a move, didn't he? Tried to claim you."

Instead of answering, a question blurted over my lips. "What's the program?"

Jaw bunching at the corners, his eyes narrowed, but he said, "You already know."

Acid bubbled in my throat. "He wanted to know if I'm the exception to the rule," I whispered. "If there was more than a barren desert b-between my legs. If I... If I might be"—I choked on a sob, humiliated, but unable to stop the confession—"if I might bred. For the g-good of the empire."

The captain offered no comfort. Didn't reach out and press me to his chest or dare to murmur sweetness against my temple.

He listened.

Held his silence and let me speak.

"He meant to set a claim on me," I babbled. Gaze falling to the floor, hands twisting in the billowing fabric hanging loose around my fingertips. "A second claim to supersede the first, so he could try to... try..." I hiccuped. "To breed me. That's what the program is, isn't it?" I asked, and met his eye. Vision too blurry to make out his reaction—too drained to taste his energy and know what lurked beneath the surface. "A program for Tritans. The citizens who *aren't* cursed with priestess blood."

He sighed, set the manacle down with a clatter of metal on wood, then claimed his seat behind the desk. "The birth of a priestess is as rare as that of an elite." He reached for me, then. Pulled me into his lap, and draped my thighs across his. Feet left to dangle above the ground. "Why do you think I was so thrilled to find you? An unbound priestess—an *adult*."

"They'll be children," I whispered, and let him tuck me beneath his chin. "Born into slavery."

He nodded, but that was it.

What else might be said?

We were quiet for a time. Recovering. Not thinking too hard or bothering to fight, I simply sat and absorbed his heat. Wiping at the occasional stray tear that wasn't soaked up by his shirt.

And then, "Sasha told me to pray." I inhaled, deep as I could. My lungs filled with the raw scent of him. Hitching only a little.

He chuckled, minty breath ruffling my hair. "Clever woman. We'll need all the divine intervention we can get if we're going to survive any retaliation attempt."

"Aren't you related?"

At this, he laughed outright. "Being his cousin has never helped me before. Why start today? And after my warrior priestess made an attempt on his life?" Reaching around me, he reclaimed the decanter and took one final, long draught. Corked the bottle, then asked, "You did the same thing to him? Affected his heart?"

Avoiding his eye, I nodded. "Sasha means to fix it. To save him, instead of letting me finish it."

Asher chuckled. "Well that can't be—"

A tentative knock at the door made us both jump. Our eyes snapping to the door, we turned to stare and I felt him go stiff beneath me. Muscles coiled and tense, but weak—soaked in a cold sweat and aching with fatigue.

Just as I was.

I met eyes that had gone bottomless and dark with possessive, seething rage. And unable to stop myself, I whispered what we were both thinking. "He's here."

19

___

"Asher—"

He clapped one large hand over my lips, hushing me. And then, lips pressed to my ear, he murmured, "It's not him."

I shivered, gooseflesh pimpling my skin at the sound of his voice. So low and husky. So *close*. But I glanced at the door and pressed my words into his palm. "You're sure?"

With a nod, the captain pushed me off his lap and said, simply, "He wouldn't knock."

It was hard to argue with that.

Hard to do anything, really, but sit in a heap where he'd left me. Curled on the floor in a tangle of bare limbs and twisted fabric. Watching as he stood, clung to the desk, then moved on unsteady feet to the window and peered down at the street below.

"Surrounded," he murmured, and pulled back from the window. Pinching the bridge of his nose with eyes squeezed shut, he pulled in a deep, controlled breath.

Exhaled in a steady stream.

And then, "Even with Colonel Viridian's support..." He scowled at the carpet. "It's not enough."

Just standing there was a drain. I could feel it pulling at me, even without touching his skin. The way he yearned to sit, to close his eyes and succumb to sleep where we both might recover some of the energy I'd squandered.

Another, more forceful knock sounded at the door. Impatient now. Edging toward frantic.

The muscle at the corner of his jaw jumped, and pausing only to collect his weapon from a desk drawer, the captain moved to answer the summons.

Side arm out of sight, hidden behind his thigh.

His finger on the trigger—my veins tingling with the distant memory of pain, but not the promise.

Because there was nothing left. Not a flicker of dark magic flickering between us.

It was a bluff.

A threat that wasn't.

Dark eyes slid over his shoulder, and the captain's chin dipped. Just once, before he turned the knob...

... and revealed Alicia.

Her face all but bloodless. Fingers twisting

around and around a crumpled envelope, the plea-sure slave had her bottom lip caught between the edges of gleaming teeth. Sparkling green eyes rimmed in white gave her the appearance of a much younger woman.

"My lord," she breathed, and rushed into the room. Taking liberties. "The general's men are here. They say you're to be escorted to the harem and won't say why—"

The captain snatched the letter from her fingers and broke the seal. Inky eyes flicking over the missive as the crease between his brows grew deeper with each passing second. "Fuck," he hissed, and crushed the offensive note in a white-knuckled fist. "*Fuck!*"

"The house it—it's surrounded by armed soldiers," Alicia whispered, wringing her hands as she took in the state of the disheveled man standing before her. "My lord—what's going on?"

He exhaled a shuddering breath. "We've been summoned." Pushing past the anxious pleasure slave, he staggered across the room and set his weapon down with a clatter of metal on wood, then stooped. Helping me to stand despite the way I swayed and clung to him for aid.

"For what?" I asked, too overwrought to pay Alicia any mind.

Instead of answering, he pushed the ball of heavy cream paper into my palm, rounded the desk, and began to riffle through his drawers. A manic energy bleeding from his entire frame.

I smoothed the crinkled paper out before me.

Captain Asher Rawlings, of the North District's Special Forces,

His Royal Majesty, Octavius Cicero Tiberius, formally requests your presence to perform a live demonstration for the entertainment of the royal sibling, before the ceremonial inauguration of several young elites.
You've been selected for this honor due, in large part, to your exemplary dedication to the empire, both on and off the battlefield.
However, rumors of your extraordinary golden priestess have been heard even in the capitol, and his Majesty is eager to see what you and the girl can do.

Your attendance to this event is a requirement.

General Harper Tilcot,
North District

I swallowed the lump in my throat. Read the letter again and again, trying to make sense of the formal speech. The foreign names of men I didn't know, and most of all, the sinister tone lurking just behind the flowery words.

"The Emperor's brother," Alicia whispered, awed. Revenant, she stood over my shoulder with fingers pressed to her lips. The subtle scent of her perfumed skin enough to make me sweat. "He's *here*? But my lord," she said. "I thought you couldn't..." Sparkling green eyes flicked to my face. "Couldn't use the priestess without killing her?"

But I didn't sneer or look away.

Obsidian eyes darted up to meet my gaze—an unspoken secret passing between us. The knowledge that it was considerably more complicated than that. The consequences more dire than either of us had ever imagined.

A secret neither of us could reveal without risking our own health—if one fell, the other would follow.

"What do we do?" Alicia hissed. "The house is completely surrounded! The general's men are in the kitchen!"

Alicia squeaked at the slap of heavy hands striking the desktop. Tension rolling off him in black waves, the captain stood with feet braced wide, head hanging low. A shock of dark hair covered a dewy forehead, shoulder blades jutting up to tent the back of his shirt. And for the space of several ragged breaths, I thought he wouldn't answer.

Thought he'd reached his limit and finally cracked right down the middle.

And then, "You will do nothing," he said, enunciating each word with clear precision. "Follow orders as they've been given and draw no unnecessary attention to yourself or the others."

Cheeks heating, Alicia looked as if she meant to argue.

"Tell them we'll be down in a moment, please," he continued, and his hands curled into fists, nails scraping at the glossy desk top. "Go now. Please?" he added when it seemed the pleasure slave wouldn't obey.

Alicia, loyal to the bitter end.

Nostrils flared white, tears brimming along her lash line, Alicia nodded and turned to go. Closing the door behind her with a careful snap.

I slid the royal summons across the desktop. "What about us?"

He took a deep, steadying breath. Set that bottomless gaze to mine, his jaw flexing around several started and aborted answers.

"We need energy," I said, choosing my words with careful intention. "Energy that won't come from rest or nutrition. It's got to come from a more... reliable source. Something we can use *now*. When we need it."

"Go on then, empath," he spat. "Say it. Out loud."

Brows raised, I merely blinked at the man whose hands were stained with the blood of a thousand slaves.

"Which one did you have your eye on, hmm?" He flung a hand out, toward the door. "Alicia for betraying your priestess blood? What about Beau?" he asked, eyes gone dark as pitch. "She's old anyway. No one will notice her missing, right?"

I shrugged. "Neither of them have the sort of power we need." Shameless in my assessment, because he knew damn-well I was right.

"Ah. You want an elite, is that it? Get a little vengeance before some magnificent last stand?"

A smirk creased the edge of my lips, and I flashed him the point of modified canines. "Can you blame me?"

"I say we take a priestess or two," he retorted, not moved by my morbid sense of humor. "Give them freedom before death."

"What's *your* solution, Captain Rawlings?" I asked, too tired to rise to the bait. Too stubborn to simply walk into the maw of death without any real effort to avoid it.

To this, he had nothing to say. Nothing but a deepening scowl and a jaw that worked around a mouth full of nothing.

I jerked my chin at the royal summons. "What is a live demonstration?"

"It's an execution. The public slaying of an enemy to the empire." He lifted one shoulder and didn't blink. "A captured rebel soldier."

"That's sick," I whispered.

"No more macabre than draining a fellow energy wielder to save ourselves."

Swallowing the retort, I said, "And this is what you people call entertainment? Amusing enough to bring some fancy royal man here to watch a defenseless soldier die?"

"Not usually," he said, and smirked. "No."

I collapsed into the chair and pulled the summons toward me once more. Seeing without reading. My eyes flicked over the scrawling loops and elegant curls of ink on crumpled paper. "Then what's different now?"

"You." And with all the subtly of a coiled predator, he added, "The sort of power I can wield with a priestess who isn't. A so-called empath. The empire is *very* interested to know what sort of tactical capabilities might come of my bond. If it can be replicated without slaughtering our stock of priestesses."

What little blood remained in my cheeks drained away, leaving me dizzy with the weight of such implications. That I really *was* unequal to this game played by men born and bred for war.

"I did warn you, Mila. Not to draw attention to yourself. Not to piss off Harper or give him reason to retaliate." Rounding the desk in three rolling strides, the captain loomed above me. Fingers twisting into the locks of silver-blonde hair that had been my downfall. "This is his revenge. He knows I can't use your power without killing you."

I licked lips gone dry. "Using it will kill us both. Asher, there's *nothing* left."

"Harper *also* knows," he continued, and pulled me close, "that a refusal before the emperor's brother will get him exactly what he's wanted all along." He laughed, then, and it was a bitter, hateful thing. "I'll be stripped of my rank. My pension. *You.*"

For the first time, I blinked and saw something more than the monster. Something deeper than the elite soldier aroused by the pain he might inflict.

I couldn't name it.

Wasn't nearly ready to do more than acknowledge it existed.

So instead, I said, "Then our options are few. Embrace what I am. Unleash the empath and take an elite"—I cleared my throat—"a... priestess, or a dozen powerless citizens and *survive*. Or die trapped. Victims of Tilcot's game."

That same tentative knock rapped on the heavy oaken door. Alicia's return signaling the end of our debate.

Questions left unanswered.

Become what this horrible place demanded of its slaves—desperate and coy, whores for the slightest scrap of power—or fall.

Together.

As enemies, fucked raw by the empire.

Bound together by secrets and blood magic.

Deeply and forever.

"What do we do?" I whispered, hardly daring to give the question life.

His eyes flicked over my face. Brushed over my lips for an instant, before he met my gaze with one that threatened to swallow me whole.

And then, simply, "We pray."

20
___

As night fell, the harem came alive. A buzzing hive of activity filled to capacity, brimming with an array of fluttering, colorful silks, the main room was ringed by a battalion of men with tight jaws and deep scowls. Men in crisp black cuts whose dark eyes were turned *in*.

Elites.

Armed...

Deadly...

Their attention fixed not to the beautiful, almost nude women trained for pleasure, but to me. To Asher. My every action watched. Documented with shrewd, alertness that left me little to do but stand and be decorated by the pleasure slaves.

Leery, on edge, I kept an eye on twitchy trigger fingers and dared not breathe too deep.

And yet...

I was surrounded by power.

In the heart of a magical storm of elite energy, the empath slumbered. Too drained to fight for even a sip of that which was not mine to take. A beast held back by fear of yet another failure, unmoved by the lure of vengeance—but one who could be awoken by one Captain of Special Forces.

He ignored my every searching glance. Every attempt to catch his eye and force the decision to save ourselves from certain death.

Instead, he'd been accommodating as we'd been dressed in formal, Caledonian garb. Attended by a flock of cooing harem slaves, their perfumed oils and shelves of mysterious creams.

Head to toe black—Asher was cloaked in a long overcoat with black stitching, black buttons, and glossy black silk lining. Every line crisp. *Sharp*. The only hint of color the weapon belted around his waist. Battered and worn, it was a subtle reminder of just what he was, despite his failure to act. His experience on the field earned by years of hardship, now reduced to little more than a show that could not be enforced.

To match, I had been draped in yards of stiff black silk edged in gold. Hair washed and plaited in complicated twists that spilled down my back, I was unrecognizable from the forest creature I'd once been.

Face painted to enhance my features, Alicia had spent the time to ensure I looked nothing like myself.

Inky eyes narrowed in tight scrutiny when he saw her progress, crossed arms testing the seams of his lavish coat, he inspected me before an audience of dazzling women. "Darker," the captain said, but that was it.

My cheeks warmed at the callous assessment, and, hurt blooming in my chest, I glanced at my fingers.

"Look up," Alicia ordered, and tilted my chin back with a hooked finger. Armed with brushes and pens, with pots of kohl and a fine golden dust, she painted until my eyes began to water with the effort to remain still. Concentration creased between the fine arches of her brows.

A gentle tap on my ankle bade me to lift my foot, and for the first time since my arrival on the front lines, shoes appeared on my feet.

Sandals with black ribbons laced up my shins. Bows tied behind my knees.

"What's the point of all this?" I asked, testing the fit.

Alicia smirked, sparkling green eyes flicking up to meet my gaze for an instant before she said, "Tradition, I suppose. The Emperor's brother sent very specific orders." She shrugged, licked her thumb, and sharpened the edge of some black smudging she'd left beneath my eye. "He might be an ancient man, but he's a man nevertheless. And in my experience, men *always* appreciate a beautiful woman."

I scowled.

"Don't," she hissed, and smacked my shoulder. "You'll crease everything I've done and I won't be able to fix it." She glanced at the battalion of soldiers ringing the harem. To the streets beyond, where day was giving over to night. "We're out of time as it is, priestess."

"Thank you, Alicia," the captain murmured, and took my elbow. Guiding me away from the paints and creams. Matching my gait, step for step, as he led me toward the exit. "You look lovely," he added under his breath.

Fists clenched, I glared at the floor. Cheeks hot. "I look like a whor—"

"Warrior," he said, and cut me off. "You look like a warrior, little priestess."

To this, I had nothing to say. Nothing to offer but flushed cheeks and dizzy compliance.

There wasn't time to speak after that.

No time to ask how he planned to get us through. No privacy to pick an elite and mark him for death in our stead.

We were escorted to the city center under armed guard, and to any watching the procession, the captain and I were decorated guests of honor. Surrounded by pomp, paraded through the throngs of Caledonians waiting to watch a man die.

For *us* to kill him with our combined might.

Whispers of unusual power haunted our every step. Words spoken behind cupped palms, we were watched by many hundreds of dark eyes glittering with the sort of savagery I'd never seen in the wilds. Never even knew existed until I'd come to this place, forced to live beneath the citizens who flocked to war, drooling for the spectacle.

When we reached our destination, it was to find the city center dressed up in twinkling lights. In the heart of a crowd thick enough to boast standing room only, a dais had been erected.

Framed by dark drapery, brightened by tiny twinkling lights, and flanked on all sides by yet more soldiers, it was an alter to the night. A spectacle shrouded in mystery and undeniable beauty.

On the far side, a raised platform complete with comfortable open tents and flapping, royal insignias —one I recognized from the summons.

As one unit, our escort stopped before a set of stairs. Three little steps that would elevate us before throngs of Caledonian citizens.

Where we would die on a pedestal, consuming each other.

I swallowed the nerves, squeezed Asher's bicep, and whispered, "Give me a name."

Inky eyes flicked down, one brow raised in question.

"Use me," I said, hardly daring to move my lips.

"Unless you have a better plan. I don't want to die dressed like this."

He snorted. Jaw tight, eyes forward, and ascended without a word. Without offering so much as a hint of his plan—if one existed at all.

The general's men fell into step behind us. Reese and Aiden, weapons cocked, looking for all the spectators as if they were chaperoning someone of grave importance. As if they weren't there as a silent reminder of what was to happen this night. The price of my reckless temper a debt to be paid in blood.

And there, standing in a gentle breeze, the Head Priestess waited. Stately. Elegant. A swirl of dark silks and effortless posture, she watched the crowd without a hint of trepidation. Her face the very picture of serenity. Hands folded neatly before her. She was ringed by four elites.

As if they stood there to protect her.

From *me*.

Muscles seizing in uncontrollable shivers I balked, leaving Asher to all but drag me to her side. Grim determination set in every hard line he possessed.

A horn blared in the distance.

Signaling soldiers to flood through the crowd, to clear a generous path directly before us—a path prepared for the sort of destruction they expected Asher to display as he killed us both.

Sweat dropped down my nape. Gathering on my

brow with the weight of the onlookers, the volume of their excited chatter a deafening roar that left me swaying. Dizzy and sick.

And so, *so* empty.

So hungry…

"Asher," I whispered, eyes darting from face to face. Seeing nothing. "*Please.*"

But still, he made no move to react.

Merely guided me forward. Passing the Head Priestess and her guards without a word or a glance, he arranged me a half-step ahead of her. Left me to wait in his shadow.

Out of reach.

Two more blasts of the horn nearly saw me bolt from the stage.

One heavy, rough hand landed on my shoulder. Pinning me in place. "Easy, priestess," Reese growled from my right. And on my left, his counterpart. Aiden. Completing the ring of elite soldiers with an even six, they stood close enough that I might feel body heat and take it for the warning it was meant to be.

Breath hitching, I managed a tight nod and fought the flood of frustrated tears that threatened to humiliate me in these last moments.

They might have my life, my power, and my body, but they could only have me if I allowed it.

I'd die staring the void into submission and know

I'd fought for this. Done more good than wrong. Except...

Trembling, I tilted my chin toward the Head Priestess and found her gaze lowered.

The soldiers surrounding her stared forward without blinking. Pupils blown wide, eyes glassy and set, they formed an eerie wall of ominous, unnatural power that didn't so much as flinch when I caught their ward's eye.

I shivered at the sight of vacant dark eyes and identical postures.

"I'm... sorry," I whispered when the shock of that icy blue gaze snapped up and settled upon me. Swallowing a hard lump, I cleared my throat and tried again. "I'm sorry for my behavior. That I couldn't be taught. That there wasn't e-enough time to—"

"Eyes forward," Reese snapped, jostling me with the butt of his weapon. Careful not to touch my skin.

Behind me, the Head Priestess sighed. "There's so much you don't know, Mila. So much I could have taught you about control. Compromise... *defense*. But you're not a priestess," she murmured. "Never will be."

I couldn't help it—I flinched, wounded by the rebuke that came on the heels of my pathetic apology. And with heart in throat, I tried to swing around and face her before Reese snarled another warning.

But I knew now. That she was here to bear

witness to my end and see her prophecies about the empath made real.

Because I was nothing.

Not a weapon or a plaything.

Just a broken, empty shell.

It was then, as I strained to maintain the illusion of a well-trained slave, to be poised, that General Tilcot emerged from the throngs of Caledonian citizens. Flanked by his own elite guard, cheeks hollow. Skin waxy and gaunt—his eyes gleamed with a mania I'd never quite seen before. One that barbed me with a shock of sick trepidation when his murky brown gaze fell upon me.

And with the gait of a much healthier man, he bounded up a set of stairs on the opposite side of the stage. Followed by soldiers hauling a heavy wooden box, and a man weighed down by shackles.

An Eloran rebel.

Filthy.

Battered and broken, he shuffled along as best he could. Gaze empty of all hope, his shoulders were slumped, face void of any hint of color.

A man who knew his last minutes were upon him.

A man who would die by my hand.

"Put it there, where his royal highness will have the best view," the general ordered, and left his men to arrange the crate to his liking. And then, strides confident, he took up a position beside the captain.

Hands clasped behind his back, booming voice low enough not to be heard over the din of a ravenous crowd—but loud enough for everyone standing close to hear, "And how's my wildcat today?" Turning, he pinned me with that muddy glare laced with a poisonous smile. "Still carrying herself like a queen, I see."

"She's exactly how I wish her to be, Harper," the captain returned without so much as a hint of respect or hesitation.

"But for how much longer, I wonder?"

To this, the captain said nothing. Didn't bother himself to look at the general, and worse, didn't make a move to take from him what might keep us alive.

"His Royal Majesty is extremely interested in her potential as a breeding sow," the general went on, oozing forged charm. "But when he finds out her power is considerably more... *offensive* than we'd thought possible? Well"—he chuckled—"there's no telling what he'll do to her in the capitol. The experiments that might be run... presuming she survives, that is."

Three blasts of the horn sent a heavy shroud of anticipation over the crowd. Bringing silence thick with a thing I couldn't sense but knew was there.

Bloodlust.

I could almost taste it.

Knew exactly what it smelled like, how it sang on the wind and hit the ear *just right*...

... and Asher wouldn't take it.

He left the empath in chains and didn't blink.

I was facing the end as I had lived my life.

Alone.

All my allies turned traitor.

Surrounded by enemies.

Dressed in a sticky layer of artful lies.

From the royal pavilion, a ring of torches burst into flame. A signal that bade the general turn, leering through a waxy grin. He clapped his hands and said, "Shall we begin?"

21

"Lords and Ladies of the North District!" General Tilcot shouted, his voice booming out over the gathered audience without the aid of an amplifier. "Tonight we are honored to host his Royal Majesty Octavius Cicero Tiberius—"

Roaring, the audience welcomed the Emperor's brother and drowned the rest of the general's opening statement.

In the royal pavilion, a man stood and waved to his subjects. Hair a shocking mop of unruly white, back still strong and stiff despite his obvious age, he carried himself with the careless ease of a man accustomed to privilege.

Bowing deeply, the general and the captain both paid their respects.

"Welcome, your majesty," Tilcot continued, then

spread his arms in a sweeping arc and addressed the crowd. "Tonight is a night of triumph and celebration! A night to celebrate our promising young elites"—he flung his left hand toward a line of six young men, all pink cheeked and dressed in pristine uniforms—"and to display what marvels the future holds." Grinning, the general strode forward and wrenched the top off the wooden crate.

The sides fell away in the most theatrical display one could possibly conceive—and revealed the massive weapon Asher had used on the field. The cannon that had left the frontlines a mess of craters and dancing, elite energy.

The very same that had almost killed me once before, now set up to finish the job.

I gasped. Staggering back into the butt of Reese's weapon.

"I'll not tell you again, priestess," he growled and nudged me forward with a hard jab to my lower back.

Flashing my teeth, I turned to confront him. Reaching for the empath, for the banked fury that didn't want to die at the hands of obedient peasants.

The well was cold.

A cauldron of frost and dust.

Neutralized of all that seething, frothing acid.

Sweat beaded on my brow, the effort for so trivial a result leaving me weak and trembling in the chill evening breeze.

"This is a day of reckoning!" the general boomed, and took the prisoner by the back of his neck. Shaking the pitiful man. "A day of triumph over our enemies!"

A wall of sound crashed down upon us. The Caledonian citizens cheering and screaming with one, insatiable voice as the captive Eloran rebel was forced to his knees.

The thin crackle of a man made to beg broke through the din of the crowd—but only *just*. Enough that I could hear it. That the sound sent a tsunami of dread spilling down my nape.

Chin tucked, I squeezed my eyes shut, creasing my makeup where Alicia couldn't fix it. Fingers curled into tight, helpless balls.

And then I prayed.

The Head Priestess took a step, and her palms landed on my collarbones. A familiar grip, but this time, absent the choking haze of priestess magic needed to soothe the beast. "You know nothing of being a priestess," she murmured, lips against my ear.

"Step back, priestess," Reese growled. "Hands off the girl—"

"Yes," she returned, and patted his cheek. "Thank you, Reese. I'm sure you've got your orders, but I can assure you, I'm quite safe from Mila. Especially in the state she's in now."

Grinding my teeth, I couldn't argue. Couldn't so much as feel even a tingle of her enticing spark.

At her touch, Reese let his weapon drop. His face going slack as his pupils swallowed a chocolaty ring of color, and without a word of protest he returned to his post. Face forward.

Lips parting on a shocked gasp, I frowned.

But before I could utter a word, she said, "There's so much I could have taught you." Extending her fingers, she ran pale digits down the side of Aiden's cheek and ensnared yet another elite—I could see it now, in the sheen of glossy blank eyes. "So much potential left untapped."

All around us, the general's booming voice continued to drone, but every scrap of my attention was focused on the Head Priestess. The calm confidence that had rendered two elites obedient slaves with nothing more than a touch.

"You're *not* a priestess," she said again, and joined me on equal footing. Flanked by no less than six empty-eyed elites who moved in time with her unspoken commands. "Not trained to use your gifts, powerless without the empath as your crutch, but"—a gentle breeze caught her unbound, silver-blonde hair and sent it dancing between us—"I will not allow you to become another tool for the empire to soil."

Pure, unfiltered terror slid into my guts. Slithering in a coil that spread through my entrails, only to double back and wrap around my heart.

"Sasha, *please*," I whispered, eyes forward. Hardly

daring to look at the woman I'd once hoped might become my greatest ally. My sister in rebellion.

On the stage before us, one inaugural elite after the other stepped forward to be introduced to the royal sibling. The general read from a list of their attributes and accomplishments, before sending each of the youths back into line.

"Every priestess who has ever been," she whispered, electric blue gaze fixed to the general's face, "has the potential to become an empath. This is a secret the empire can never possess."

I nodded, quaking deep in my middle. Knowing she meant to act. That she couldn't allow me to live and compromise the rest of her flock.

The last of the young elites stepped back into line, and with a hideous grin, General Tilcot turned to the captain, and said, "And now to mark the beginning of the festivities, my own cousin, Captain Asher Rawlings of the Special Forces will use his golden priestess to usher us into a new era! One of unimaginable power brought on by a *new* generation of priestess!"

When a cool, dry palm landed on my elbow, I didn't bother to flinch. No matter the way my heart hammered in my chest, the floundering of my breath, I set my jaw and readied myself for what came next. "This is the last weapon I have left."

"She is a priestess of rare power!" the general

boomed. "One whose innate gifts have been the subject of rumor and gossip, for with a single shot"—he strode across the dais toward the weapon that would spell my doom—"the captain was able to quell a rebellion!"

"Elites are born and bred for war," the Head Priestess murmured, brow wrinkled as she watched her counterpart through a sneer. "But only a priestess can take something corrupt and make it new."

I took a shuddering breath. "I don't want to be their weapon," I whispered, blinking. And despite my best efforts, tears spilled over my lashes. Hot and salty, I was shamed before an audience of Caledonians. Weak and pathetic at the very end, no matter the frost of numb blanketing me from head to toe.

"I think you are that new thing," Sasha murmured, watching as the captain stepped forward, jaw a tight, grim line. "The priestesses are all gone. Taken and enslaved by the empire. All except *you*."

My head snapped toward her, eyes wide as I tried to pull meaning from her words. Tried to make sense of what she said, despite the way my head spun. "Sasha—I don't—"

"Pray to your heathen gods," the general spat, kicking the rebel soldier before he stooped. Hands outstretched to claim the weapon.

But she gave me no time to understand. "I've had something delivered to the captain's rooms," she said, and smiled. "I think you'll know what to do with it. That it isn't the answer for the rest of them."

She took another step—and her elites followed without a word of command. Claimed puppets, absent any hint of self-preservation or individual thought, they followed.

Each one offering up a flood of unimaginable power for her to redirect. To make new.

The general's hands landed on sleek metal.

A trap snapped shut.

Sasha's veins lit with a blinding gold. Flooded in the space it took me to stumble forward, a warning bursting from my lips.

Too late.

Forearms bunched with corded muscle, the general cried out. Unable to drop the cannon that surged with a blaze of poisonous green fire. Charging with a high-pitched squeal that warned of too much power, surging too fast.

A blazing goddess dressed in cleansing blue flames, Sasha merely continued her advance. Her elites a tight *V* of protection and sacrifice, they were a perfect contrast to her magnificence—they were drained of their vitality. Their magic gobbled up by a master, sent to kill a general.

And there, beneath the skin of powerful men, Sasha's elites showed the strain.

Their veins turned black before my eyes.

"No!" I screamed, stumbling after her. Inhaling

the scent of baking flesh, I gagged. "Sasha! Please don't!"

Bellowing his rage, the general spun, splashing arcs of plasma all over the wooden dais.

Seared by the intensity of that sickly glow, I tried to squeeze my eyes shut—and found I could see even through the darkness behind my lids.

I charged forward anyway, flinging one bent arm over my eyes. "Sasha!"

"Let there be nothing but dust."

The words echoed around the platform. Ethereal and without tether, they came from her lips but were heard above the screams of noble women. Louder even than the panicked cries of men hollering for order, and a general holding the reins of an explosion he simply could not hope to match.

Outnumbered seven to one, he lost control.

Belching thick waves of incandescent plasma, the weapon misfired.

A hard body collided with my ribs, sending us both crashing to the ground in a breathless heap.

I felt him, then.

His weight pinned me down, guarding me against the waves of heat that set fire to the stage and ate through a swath of Caledonian citizens in a single, burning instant.

Asher.

"Help her!" I screamed, straining to throw him off.

The general collapsed, swallowed by his own

ambition, his legs simply... burnt away, nothing left behind but a greasy film that coated my skin. My tongue and sinuses.

But Sasha—she *shone*.

Veins lit with blue fire—with pure priestess magic—she wielded the energy of six elites and put an end to General Harper Tilcot.

Taking her vengeance, her spine arched. Bowing back at an impossible angle, her jaws parted on a soundless scream. Hair whipping around her in a storm of her own making, she showed me what a priestess really was, before they'd all gone extinct.

Draining her elites to kill a general, she turned them to char.

Awed, I watched them crumble. Couldn't so much as blink when their bones were turned to ash, their eyes and flesh flaking, carried off as dust on the breeze.

Disappeared as if they never were.

Only she remained.

Broken but unbent.

The very last of Tritan's priestesses.

Thank you for reading *Frost to Dust, The Last Tritan*, book II. Flip the page for a full chapter preview of book III, *Dust to Smoke*!

If you like *free things, sneak peaks, giveaways, and super secret news about future projects*, then boiii is there a place for you! Tis called The Daniverse, and you can join by searching for "The Daniverse, by Myra Danvers" on Facebook.

DUST TO SMOKE

She was dying.

I could feel it on the wind.

Could see it in the quiet glow still flickering in her veins, where dying embers glowed a soft, gentle blue in muscles with nothing left to give.

It was there, in the pull behind my ribs, where she'd touched me with her gifts. Where she'd built protection I had thought to be a trap. Blinded by my helpless fury.

My impotent, boundless rage.

And now it was too late.

The Head Priestess couldn't be saved from the bone chilling void.

Still, I reached for her. Crushed beneath the protective weight of a possessive male, I extended one trembling hand and took her ankle in hand. Wrapped it in fingers grimy with soot—stained by the ashen remains of the elites she'd sent to escort her into the void—and threw everything I had into the abyss.

To bring her back.

Fueling her dying body with what little remained of my corrupt gifts.

"*Mila.*"

It was a warning in a voice I didn't quite hate.

One I ignored as I wilted beneath his weight, faltering with the effort needed to sustain her broken shell when I had so little to left give. Desperate to hold her here, on this side of the veil.

Where I *needed* her.

Where I could apologize for the hurt I'd caused.

Chaos reigned all around me. The screams of the dying and ruined a haunting symphony wailing tribute to the power of Tritan's last true priestess.

Flames, flickering with a poisonous green, consumed the podium that was supposed to be our final stand. Sluggish, but hot enough to crisp the cheeks of any daring enough to get too close.

I felt nothing.

Nothing but the dusting of frost, the cold where she'd gone... where I meant to follow...

"*Mila, stop.*"

I couldn't. Not now, with her lips tinged blue. Her chest so still.

A warm, calloused palm caressed my cheek, lips moving against my ear. "You have to let her go."

It was cruel to ask for such a thing when I hadn't given everything I could in the attempt to save her.

"There's nothing more you can do."

At this, a wordless sound of pain and denial crackled over my lips. Aggravating the blisters lining my throat, where I'd inhaled the searing heat of her final moments. The dust and smoke of her doomed escort.

Long fingers carded through my hair, soothing, despite the catch of callouses that pulled at my scalp. "Let her go before she takes you with her, little warrior. Before she takes us both."

My grip tightened around that slender ankle. Nails biting into flesh growing cold and spongy, dimpled in a way that seemed unable to bounce back. Still, I held on despite the way the cold spread. "I... don't care..."

Lips pressed to the corner of my jaw, the rasp of his beard prickled against my ear. "Your fight isn't over," he murmured and caught my jaw. Turning my eyes away from the woman I'd failed, he ensnared me with an unblinking stare. Trapped me in twin pools of swirling, inky depths.

A primal call to arms, he dared me to fight. Issued a challenge in a language I couldn't speak but couldn't ignore.

Anguish splintered through my chest, and I sobbed, torn right down the middle. Brushing up against her spirit, just once more, before he reeled me in. Allowed a single, silent farewell, before he pulled me back from the edge with the reins I no longer held.

She slipped away, fading into nothingness so quickly and irrevocably, that for a moment I wasn't sure if she'd ever really existed at all.

"She's gone."

It was spoken in a voice thick with pain. One I didn't recognize as mine or his.

He brushed a lock of tangled hair back from my face, careful where it stuck to tear-stained cheeks. Patient, he was content to wait, ignoring the flames and the chaos.

And to my horror, a flood of tears washed over my lashes—I saw it in the reflection of eyes gone dark as pitch. "She... she *killed* herself," I rasped, eyes wide. Reeling, my hairline growing damp and itchy. "Killed them all."

"I know," he whispered, and traced the delicate angles made wet with shock, brushing at the deluge of tears that tracked down my cheeks and cleansed me of the soot of the dead.

"It was a trap. The"—I whined—"the instant he touched th-that cannon, h-he—" Traumatized, gut wrenching sobs broke through my illusion of inner strength.

Hushing me, he sat back and pulled me into his lap, cradling my cheek tight against his chest, where my tears were hidden from the hordes of frantic Caledonians trying to escape. Where they might dry against his skin and couldn't be burned away by the heat of Sasha's final stand. "She knew what she was doing."

The offer of comfort bought only another flood of pitiful anguish, and I clung to him.

My enemy.

Fingers winding tight into the sodden fabric of his formal wear—gritty with a dusting of unspeakable grime—my lips moved of their own volition. "She died an empath," I murmured, quiet enough that I wasn't sure he heard my confession. "And I gave her the idea. It was my fault," I whispered, and it echoed all around us with the ring of truth.

Grab your copy of *Dust to Smoke* today!

ALSO BY MYRA DANVERS

Swallowed by Darkness ~ FREE

https://dl.bookfunnel.com/htwvlecj86

The Last Tritan

- Flame to Frost, The Last Tritan, Book I
- Frost to Dust, The Last Tritan, Book II
- Dust to Smoke, The Last Tritan, Book III

Tritan Evolution

- Ravenous Innocence, Tritan Evolution, Book I
- Insatiable Corruption, Tritan Evolution, Book II
- Lavish Destruction, Tritan Evolution, Book III

The Feral Court

- Renegade, the Feral Court, Book I
- Giaus, The Feral Court, Book II
- Sickle, The Feral Court, Book III

Atom and Evil

- Delirium, Atom and Evil, Book I

MYRA DANVERS

USA Today Bestselling author, Myra Danvers, is best known for her compelling mix of unique science fiction and dark fantasy worlds that feature feisty heroines, antihero men, and of course, proper villains. Though you may not always know who is who until the final pages...

facebook.com/MyraDanvers

instagram.com/myradanvers

bookbub.com/profile/myra-danvers

goodreads.com/MyraDanvers